Hjalmar Hjorth Boyesen

Gunnar

A tale of Norse life. Fourth Edition

Hjalmar Hjorth Boyesen

Gunnar
A tale of Norse life. Fourth Edition

ISBN/EAN: 9783337016012

Printed in Europe, USA, Canada, Australia, Japan

Cover: Foto ©Andreas Hilbeck / pixelio.de

More available books at **www.hansebooks.com**

GUNNAR

A TALE OF NORSE LIFE

BY

HJALMAR HJORTH BOYESEN

Fourth Edition.

NEW YORK
CHARLES SCRIBNER'S SONS
743 & 745 BROADWAY
1880

TO

IVAN S. TOURGUÉNEFF,

WITH THE LOVE, GRATITUDE, AND REVERENCE

OF

THE AUTHOR.

CONTENTS.

GUNNAR : A NORSE ROMANCE.

I.

THE LAKE.

FAR up under the snow-line, where the sun seldom rises, and, when it rises, seldom sets, is a lake. In the long summer days, grave fir-trees and barren rocks, wearing on their brows the wrinkles of centuries, reflect their rugged heads in its mirror; but it is not often that gentle spring and summer find their way hither on their wanderings round the earth, and when they do, their stay is brief. And again winter blows his icy breath over the mountains; stiff and dead lie the waters, and the

1*

fir-trees sigh under the burden of the heavy snow.

At the northern end of the lake, the Yokul, the son of winter, lifts his mighty head above the clouds, and looks in cold contempt down upon the world below; with his arms, the long, freezing glaciers, he embraces the landscape around him, hugging it tightly to his frosty bosom.

On the eastern side the rocks open wide enough for a little brook to escape from the mountains into the valley; and as it runs chattering between the ferns and under the tree-roots, it tells them from year to year an endless tale of the longings of the lake and of the despotic sway of the stern old Yokul. But once every year, when spring comes with merry birds and sunshine, the little brook feels itself larger and stronger, and it swells with joy, and bounds laughing over the crooked tree-roots, and throws in its wantonness a kiss of good-by to its old friends, the ferns. Every spring the brook is glad; for it knows it will join the river, it knows it will reach the ocean.

"The flood is coming," said the old people in

the valley, and they built a dam in the opening of the rocks, where the brook had flowed, and stopped it. Farther down they put up a little mill with a large water-wheel, which had years ago belonged to another mill, so that the whole now looked like a child with its grandfather's hat and spectacles on.

"Now we will make the brook of some use," said they; and every time the lake rose to the edge of the dam, they opened the flood-gate; the water rushed down on the mill, the water-wheel turned round and round, and the mill-stones ground the grain into flour. So the brook was made of use.

But up on the mountain the snow lay deep yet, and the bear slept undisturbed in his wintry cave. Snow loaded the branches of the pines, and the ice was cold and heavy on the bosom of the lake. For spring had not yet come there; it always came first to the old folks down in the valley. It was on its way now up the mountain-side.

A mild breeze stole over the rocks and through

the forest; the old fir shook her branches and rose upright. Masses of snow fell down on the rock; they rolled and grew, as they rolled, until with a heavy thump they reached the lake. A loud crash shot through the ice from shore to shore.

A few sunbeams came straggling in through the forest, struck the fir, and glittered on the ice, where the wind had swept it bare.

"Spring is coming," said the old tree, doubting whether to trust her own eyes or not; for it was long since she had seen the spring. And she straightened herself once more, and shook her tough old branches again.

"Spring is coming," she repeated, still speaking to herself; but the stiff pine, standing hard by, heard the news, and she told it to the birch, the birch to the dry bulrushes, and the bulrushes to the lake.

"Spring is coming," rustled the bulrushes, and they trembled with joy. The lake heard it, and its bosom heaved; for it had longed for the spring. And the wind heard it, and whispered the message of joy, wherever it came, to the rocks, to the glaciers, and to the old Yokul. "Spring is coming," said the wind.

And the lake wondered; for it thought of the swallows of last spring, and of what the swallows had said. "Far from here," chirped the swallows, "is the great ocean; and there are no pine-trees there, no firs to darken the light of the sun, no cold and haughty Yokul to freeze the waters."

"No firs and no Yokul?" said the lake, wondering, for it had never seen anything but the firs and the Yokul.

"And no rocks to bound the sight and hinder the motion," added the swallows.

"And no rocks!" exclaimed the lake; and from that time it thought of nothing but the ocean.

For two long years the lake had been thinking, until at last it thought it would like to tell somebody what it had been thinking; the old fir looked so wise and intelligent, it felt sure that the fir would like to know something about the ocean. But then it wondered again what it had to tell the fir about the ocean, and how it should tell it, until at last spring came, and it had not yet spoken. Then the fir spoke.

"What are you thinking about?" said the fir.

"About the ocean," answered the lake.

"The ocean!" repeated the fir, in a tone of inexpressible contempt; "what is the use of thinking about the ocean? Why don't you think of the mill?"

"Have you ever seen the ocean?" asked the lake, timidly.

"Seen the ocean? No; but I have seen the mill, and that is a great deal better." And the fir shrugged her great shoulders, as if pitying both the ocean and those that could waste a thought on it.

Then for a long time the lake was silent, until it felt that it could no longer hold its peace; then it spoke. This time, it thought it would speak to the pine; the pine was younger and might perhaps itself once have had longings for the ocean.

"Have you ever longed for the ocean?" said the lake to the pine.

"I have longed for the mill," answered the pine, harshly, and its voice sounded cold and shrill; "and that is what you had better long for too," it added. The pine looked down into the clear water, and saw its own image; it shook its stately branches and seemed greatly pleased with its own appearance.

"But," began the lake again, "would you not like to see the ocean?"

"No," cried the pine, "my father and my father's father grew up, lived, and died here; they never saw the ocean, and they were just as well off without it. What would be the use of seeing the ocean?"

"I do not know," sighed the lake, and was silent; and from that time it never spoke about the ocean, but it thought the more of it, and longed for the spring and the swallows.

It was early in June. The sun rose and shone warm on the Yokul, night and day. To the lake it seldom came, only now and then a few rays would go astray in the forest, peep forth between the rugged trunks, and flash in the water; then hope swelled in the bosom of the lake, and it knew that spring was coming.

At last came spring, and with it the sea-winds and the swallows. And every evening, when the sun shone red and dreamy, the lake would hear the sea-wind sing its strange songs about the great ocean, and about the tempests that lifted its waves to the sky; it would listen to the swallows, as they told their wonder-stories of the blooming lands beyond the ocean, where there were no firs, no rocks, and no Yokul, but in their stead palm-trees with broad glittering leaves and sweet fruits, beautiful gardens and sunshiny hills, looking out over the great boundless ocean.

"And," said the swallows, "there is never any snow and ice there; always light and sunshine."

"Always light and sunshine?" asked the lake, wondering; and its thoughts and its longings grew toward the great ocean and that sunshiny land beyond it.

The sun rose higher and shone on the Yokul warmer than ever before; the Yokul sparkled and glittered in the sunshine; it was almost merry, for it smiled at the sun's trying to melt it.

"It is no use trying," said the Yokul; "I have been standing here so long now, that it is of no use trying to change me." But change it did, although it was too stubborn to own it; for it sent great swelling rivers down its sides, down into the valley and into the lake.

And as the sun rose, the lake grew; for there was strength in the sunshine. The old fir shook her head, and shrugged her shoulders; but still the lake kept growing, growing up over her feet, until the old fir stood in the water above her knees. Then she lost her patience.

"What in all the world are you thinking about?" exclaimed the old tree.

"About the ocean," said the lake; "O that I could see the ocean!"

"Come," whispered the sea-wind, dancing down over the mountain-side, "come to the ocean."

"Come," chirped the swallows, "come to the ocean."

"I am coming," said the lake, and it rushed

upon the dam; the barrier creaked and broke.
The lake drew a full breath, and onward it leaped,
onward over the old mill, which tottered and fell;
onward through fields and meadows, through forests and plains; onward it rushed, onward to the
ocean.

II.

· HENJUMHEI.

HERE the valley is narrowest, the mountain steepest, and the river swiftest, lies Henjumhei. The cottage itself is small and frail, and smaller and frailer still it looks with that huge rock stooping over it, and the river roaring and foaming below; it seems almost ready to fall. The river, indeed, seems to regard it as an easy prey; for every spring, when it feels lusty and strong, it draws nearer and nearer to the cottage, flings its angry foam in through the narrow window-holes, and would perhaps long ago have hurled the moss-grown beams down over its brawling rapids, if it had not been for the old rock, which always frowns more sternly than ever when the river draws too near the cottage. Perhaps it was the same fear of the river which

induced Gunnar Thorson Henjumhei, Thor Gunnarson's father, to plant two great beams against
the eastern and western walls; there is now but
little danger of its falling, and Thor Gunnarson
has lived there nearly ten years since his father,
Gunnar, felled that great fir, which felled himself,
so that he had to be brought home to die. Now,
how old Gunnar, who was known to be the best
lumberman in all the valley, could have managed
to get that trunk over his neck, was a matter
which no one pretended to understand, except
Gunhild, his widow; and every one knew that she
was a wise woman. This was what she said : —

"There was an old fir, the finest mast that ever
struck root on this side the mountains; but the
tree was charmed, and no one dared to fell it : for
it belonged to the Hulder,* and it was from the

---

* The Hulder is a kind of personification of the forest;
she is described as a maiden of wonderful beauty, and only in
this respect different from her mortal sisters, that she has a
long cow's-tail attached to her beautiful frame. This is the
grief of her life. She is always longing for the society of mor-
tals, often ensnares young men by her beauty, but again and
again the tail interferes by betraying her real nature. She is
the protecting genius of the cattle.

top of that old fir that she called with her loor *
her herds of motley cattle; many a time she had
been seen sitting there at eventide, counting her
flocks, and playing her mournful loor until not a
calf or a kid was missing. No man had dared to
fell the tree, for it would have been that man's
death. Then there came one day a lumber-mer-
chant from town; he saw the mast and offered
two hundred silver dollars for it. Old Lars Henjum said he might have it, if he could find the
man who had the courage to fell it. Now, that
thing was never made which Gunnar was afraid
of, and he would like to see the woman, said he,
either with tail or without it, who could scare
him from doing what he had made up his mind to
do. So he felled the mast, and paid with his life
for his boldness. For behind the mast stood the
Hulder, and it was not for nothing that the last
stroke of the axe brought the huge trunk down
on the lumberman's head. Since then ill luck

* The loor is a straight birch-bark horn, widening toward
one end. It is from three to six feet long, and is used for
calling the cattle home at evening.

has ever followed the family, and ever will follow it," said old Gunhild.

Before his father's death Thor Henjumhei had been the first dancer and the best fighter in all the valley. People thought him a wild fellow, and the old folks shrugged their shoulders at his bold tricks and at his absurd ideas of going to sea to visit foreign countries, or of enlisting as a soldier and fighting in unknown worlds. Why did he not, like a sensible man, marry and settle down as his father and his father's father 'had done before him, and work like them for his living, instead of talking of the sea and foreign countries? This puzzled the good old folks considerably; but in spite of their professed dislike for Thor, they could never help talking about him; and, in spite of all his wildness, they could not help owning that there really was something about him which made even his faults attractive. Strange it was, also, that, although Thor was only a houseman's * son, many a gardman's wife had

* In the rural districts of Norway there is sharp distinction between a "gardman," or a man who owns his land, and

been seen smiling graciously upon him when her fair daughter was leaning on his arm in the whirling spring-dance. But since the day he had found his father in the forest, bloody and senseless, under the Hulder's fir, no one recognized in him the old Thor. He settled down in the little cottage by the river, married according to his mother's wish, worked as hard and as steadily as a plough-horse, and nevermore mentioned the sea or foreign countries. Old Gunhild was happier than ever; for, although she had lost her husband (poor soul, anybody might have known that he would come to a sudden end), she had found her son. And as for Birgit, her daughter-in-law, she was the gentlest and most obedient creature that ever was, and did exactly as Gunhild bade her; thus they lived together in peace and unity, and were not even known to have had a single quarrel, which is a most remarkable circumstance, considering that they were daughter-in-

a "houseman," who pays the rent of his house and an adjoining piece of land large enough to feed a cow or two, by working a certain number of weeks or months a year for the gardman.

law and mother-in-law, and lived under the same roof and even in the same room. But Birgit had as firm a belief in Gunhild's superiority of sense and judgment as she had in the old silver-clasped Bible or in Martin Luther's Catechism, and would no more have thought of questioning the one than the other. Her husband she had never known in his wild days, and although she had heard people tell about the gay and daring lad, who could kick the rafter in the loftiest ceiling, and on whose arm the proudest maiden was fain to rest, she somehow never could persuade herself to believe it. To her he always remained the stern, silent Thor, to whom she looked up with an almost reverential admiration, and whose very silence she considered the most unmistakable proof of superior wisdom.

Nearly a year had Birgit been at Henjumhei, and Christmas came round again. It was on Christmas eve that Gunnar Thorson was born; for of course the boy was christened Gunnar, after his grandfather. Thor came home late from the woods that night. Gunhild was standing in the door, looking for him.

"It is cold to-night, mother," said he, pulling off his bear-skin mittens, and putting his axe up in its old place under the roof.

"You may well say so, son," said Gunhild.

Thor fixed an inquiring look on his mother's face. She read the look, and answered it before he had time to ask.

"A boy," said she, "a beautiful child."

"A boy," repeated Thor, and his stern features brightened as he spoke. He took off his cap before he went in that night. Gunhild followed.

"Wonderful child, indeed," said she, "born on a Christmas eve." Then she went out again, took a large knife, polished it until it shone like silver, and stuck it with the point in the door.

"Now, thank God," muttered she to herself, "the child is safe and no hill-people* will dare to change it."

Days came and days went, and a month had

---

* The hill-people are a kind of ugly pygmies with big heads and small bodies. They often steal new-born infants and place their own in the plundered cradle. Such changelings have large glassy eyes with a blank stare, and eat immensely, but never grow very large, and can never learn to speak.

passed. The child grew, and the mother failed; and every night when Thor came home from his work he looked more and more troubled. Gunhild saw it.

"When spring has crossed the mountains, she will get well," said she.

But spring came; the sun shone bright and warm on the Yokul and the western glaciers; the icy peaks reflected its light into the narrow valley, and the Yokul sparkled like a crystal palace.

"Now spring is coming," said Gunhild.

It was early in June, and spring's first flower came just in time to adorn Birgit's coffin. All the neighbors were at the funeral; and no man who saw the dense crowd in the churchyard would have supposed that this was the funeral of a houseman's wife. When the ceremony was over, the pastor came up to shake hands with Thor and Gunhild.

"A hard loss, Thor," said the pastor.

"A hard loss, father," said Thor.

"Unexpected?"

"Unexpected. Mother thought spring would

make her well." His lip quivered, and he turned abruptly round.

"And spring did make her well, Thor," said the pastor, warmly, grasping Thor's hand and giving it a hearty parting shake.

If the cottage of Henjumhei had ever seen such wild deeds as it did while that boy was growing up, it surely must have been very long ago. For there was no spot from the chimney-top to the cellar to which he did not scramble. "And it certainly is a wonder," said his grandmother, "that he does not break his neck, and tear the house down ten times a day." The cottage contained only one room, with an open hearth in a corner, and two beds, one above the other, both built between the wall and two posts reaching from the floor to the roof. There was no ceiling, but long smoky beams crossing the cottage. A few feet above these were nailed a dozen boards or more, crosswise from one rafter in the roof to another on the opposite side. This is called Hemsedal, or the bed where strangers sleep. There the beggar and the wanderer may always

find a sack of straw and a bed of pine branches
whereon to rest their weary limbs. These beams
were Gunnar's special delight. He was not many
years old, before he could get up there by climbing the door; each beam had its own name from
stories which his grandmother had told him, and
he sat there and talked with them for hours
together. On the one nearest the hearth was an
old saddle which had been hanging there from
immemorial times; its name was "Fox," and on
it he rode every day over mountains, seas, and
forests to free the beautiful princess who was
guarded by the Trold with three heads.

In the winter, as soon as the short daylight
faded, he would spend hours in Hemsedal; and
to his grandmother's inquiry about what he was
doing there, he would always answer that he was
looking at the dark. Although Gunhild never
liked to have the boy sit up there, and often was
herself frightened at the strange things he said,
she never dared bid him come down; for her
superstition peopled the cottage as well as all
nature around her with elves and fairy spirits,

whom she would not for any price offend. They might, indeed, some time in the boy's life, prove a potent protection to him.

There was only one thing which Gunnar liked better than riding Fox and looking at the dark, and that was to listen to grandmother's stories; for grandmother could tell the most wonderful stories. Thor was very fond of his son, but it was not his way to show his fondness, and still less to speak of it; but, though nothing was said, it was always understood that he wished to have the boy near him in the evening when the day's work was done. Then he would light his old clay-pipe, and take his seat on one side of the hearth; on the low hearth-stone itself his mother would sit, and little Gunnar on the floor between them. It was on such evenings, while Thor was busily smoking and carving some wooden box or spoon, and grandmother knitting away on her stocking, that she would tell her stories about Necken,* who had loved in vain, and plays his

* As the Hulder is the spirit of the forest, so Necken is the spirit of the water. He lives in the wildest cataracts, where

sad tunes in the silent midsummer night; much she knew also of the Hulder, whose beauty is greater than mortal eye ever beheld. But the finest story of all was the one about the poor boy who walked thousands of miles, through endless forests and over huge mountains, to kill the Trold, and free the beautiful princess. Gunnar never could weary of that story, and grandmother had to tell it over and over again.

One night Gunhild had just told of the boy and the princess for the third time. The fire on the hearth threw its red lustre upon the group. There was no candle or lamp in the room, only a drowsy stick of fir flickered from a crevice in the wall. Gunnar sat staring into the dying embers. . "What are you staring at, boy?" said his father.

"O father, I see the Trold, and the boy, and the princess, and all of them, right there in the fire," cried Gunnar, eagerly.

he plays his violin, or, according to others, a harp, and he who listens closely may hear his wonderful music above the roaring of the water.

"You had better go to bed," said Thor.

Now Gunnar would have liked to hear something more about the poor boy, but he durst not disobey; so he reluctantly climbed up to his grandmother's bed, undressed, and went to sleep. But that night he dreamed that the cottage was an enchanted palace, that his grandmother was an enchanted princess, and his father the three-headed Trold who kept the charm. The next morning he cautiously suggested the idea to his grandmother, whom he frightened so thoroughly that she promised herself never in her life to tell the child any Trold-story again. And she never did. But the story had made too deep an impression upon the boy's mind ever to be forgotten. He tried repeatedly to learn more from his grandmother about the later fate of the poor boy and the princess; but the grandmother always lost her temper whenever he approached that subject, and stubbornly refused to satisfy his thirst for knowledge. Then he determined to make explorations at his own risk; for he knew it would be of no use asking his father. There must surely be more than one beautiful princess in the world, thought he, and more than one Trold too; and he knew a boy who would not be afraid to meet any number of Trolds, for the sake of one beautiful princess.

Few people ever came to Henjumhei, for it was very much out of the way, being far from the church-road, and the river was too swift to be crossed so far up. Farther down the current was not so strong, and there a skilful boatman could row across without danger. Now and then a beggar would find his way up to the cottage, and, as these visits brought many bits of pleasant gossip and parish news, and, moreover, formed Gunhild's only connection with the world outside, through the long dark winter, they were always gratefully accepted, and the visitor never went away unrewarded. Of course Thor never knew of what was going on in the valley, and every girl in the parish might have married, and every other man emigrated, for all he cared. He had enough to do with his own affairs, he said, and so had his neighbor with his. This was a point of constant disagreement between Gunhild and her son; for she was naturally of a social disposition, and led this lonely life more from necessity than from choice. As for Gunnar, he knew nothing about the people in the valley, and consequently felt no interest in them; but still he enjoyed the visits of the beggars as much as his grandmother; he always looked upon them with a kind of reverential awe, and would not have been in the least surprised if he had seen their rags suddenly turn into gold and purple. The boy had lived so long in a world of his own imagination, and had had so very little to do with the world of reality, that he was not able to distinguish the one from the other.

III.

THE GARDMAN FOLKS.

BOUT a mile down the river, where the valley opens widely toward the fjord and the sunshine, lies Henjum, the largest estate within hundreds of miles. Atle Larsson Henjum is the first man in the whole parish, and even the pastor himself pays him his regular visits after the Christmas and Easter offerings. In church he always takes the foremost seat, nearest the pulpit, and the pastor seldom commences his sermon before Atle is in his seat. On offering-days he is always the first man at the altar. Atle Henjum is only a peasant, but he is proud of being a peasant. "My father and my father's father, and again his father, as far back as Saga records, were peasants," he would say, "so I do not see why I should wish to be anything else."

Atle always likes to speak of his father and his
father's father, and he is sure never to think of
doing anything which they have not done before
him. It is because his father always had occupied the foremost seat in church that he feels
bound to do it; as for himself, it makes no differ-
ence to him where he sits. Everybody who could
remember Lars Atleson, Atle's father, said that
never had a son followed more closely in father's
footsteps than Atle did. As far back in time as
memory goes, Atle's ancestors had lived on Henjum, and their names had been alternately Lars
Atleson and Atle Larsson; consequently, when
Atle's son was born, he would probably rather
have drowned him than given him any other
name than Lars.

Henjum holds as commanding a position over
the rest of the valley as its lord over his fellow-
parishioners. The fresh-painted, red, two-story
building, with its tall chimneys and slated roof,
looks very stately indeed on the gently sloping
hillside, with the dark pine forest behind it and
the light green meadows below.

Atle Henjum owned a good deal more land
than he could take care of himself; more than
half of his estate he leased to his housemen, in
lots large enough to hold a cottage and feed one
or two cows. These housemen, of which Thor
Henjumhei was one, paid the lease of their land
by working a certain number of weeks on the
"gard," as they called the estate to which they
and their lots belonged. Atle himself was thus
called the gardman, and his family the gardman
folks.

Atle's father and father's father had been hard
workers, and so was Atle himself; and the houseman who expected to remain long in his service
must follow his example; next, he must have no
will of his own, but do exactly as he was told,
without saying one word for or against. To this
last rule, however, there was one exception; Thor
Henjumhei was a man of as few words as his
master, but of all the housemen he was the only
one who was allowed to speak his opinion, or,
more, who was requested to do so. There was a
singular kind of friendship between the two,

founded on mutual respect. Atle knew well that
Thor was as stiff and at bottom as proud as himself, and Thor had the same conviction with regard to Atle. Seldom was any new land broken,
a fallow field sown, or a lumber bargain settled,
before Thor's opinion was heard.

Atle Henjum had two children. Lars, the boy,
was by two years the older; he was of just the
same age as Thor's son, Gunnar. The daughter's
name was Gudrun.

The Henjum estate stretched straight to the
river, on either side of which was a boat-house,
one belonging to Henjum, and the other to Rimul.
Rimul was a large and fine estate, though not
quite as large as Henjum; the house was only one
story, and did not look half as stately as the big
Henjum building; but it had such a friendly and
cheerful look about it, that nobody could help
wishing to step in, when he chanced to pass by.
Ingeborg Rimul herself was the stateliest woman
you might see; indeed, she was not Atle Henjum's
sister for nothing. Atle had never had more than
this one sister, and while she was at home he had

always been proud of her stately growth and fair appearance. Of course Ingeborg had a suitor for every finger, while she was a maiden; but when anybody asked her why none of the young lads found favor with her (and there were many mothers of promising sons who put that question to her), she always answered that she was in no hurry. Then one day a young man from the city came to visit the parsonage. He had studied for the ministry at the University of Christiania, wore a long silk tassel in his cap, and spectacles on his nose. His name was Mr. Vogt. He had not been long in the valley before he discovered in church a girl with long golden hair and a pair of eyes which interested him exceedingly. Ingeborg received many invitations from the parsonage in those days, even so many that Atle began to suspect mischief, and forbade her going there altogether. Ingeborg of course dared not disobey her brother. She never went to the parsonage again while Mr. Vogt was there. But somebody thought he had seen a long silk tassel and a pair of bright blue eyes down on the shore late one dreamy summer evening; and another, who thought he had seen more, was not sure but it was fair Ingeborg's golden head he had recognized resting on Mr. Vogt's bosom one moonlight night, under the great birch-tree by the river. Whether true or not, sure it was that all the valley was talking about it; but strange to say, the last to hear it and the last to believe it was Atle Henjum. In fact, it made him so angry, when somebody congratulated him on his new brother-in-law, that no one from that day dared mention Vogt's name in his presence. But Atle also had his eyes opened before long. For one day Mr. Vogt came marching up the hills to Henjum, and asked to see Atle. What passed between them no one ever knew : all that was known is that Mr. Vogt left the parsonage that very night, and went back to the city; that Ingeborg, against her custom, did not appear either at church or anywhere else for several weeks, and that the next time she did appear, people thought she looked a little paler, and carried her head somewhat higher than usual. Before the year passed she was married to Sigurd Rimul, who was

several years younger than herself. Atle made
the wedding, and a grand wedding it was; it lasted from Wednesday till Monday; there was drink-
ing and dancing, and both pastor and judge were
invited. Never had a bride on this side of the
mountains brought such a dowry; there was wool
and linen and silver enough to cover the road
from the church to the bridal-house; so she had
every reason to feel happy, and, if she did not, it
was not her fault, for she tried hard. Since that
time Mr. Vogt was never seen, and seldom heard
of in the valley. The parson told somebody who
asked for him, that he had married a wealthy
man's daughter, and was settled as pastor of a
large parish near the city.

It was now about seven or eight winters since
Ingeborg's wedding; if she had not known sorrows before, as indeed she had, her married life
did not begin with too bright a prospect. Sigurd
was a good husband; so everybody said, and no
one was readier to praise him than his wife.
People said, however, that Ingeborg still had
everything her own way, and that Sigurd had " to

dance to his wife's pipe." But if anybody had
dared hint such a thing in Sigurd's presence, there
is no knowing what he might have done; for, kind
and gentle as he was, the saying was, that he had
one tender point, and when any one touched that
he was wilder than a bear. Sigurd was proud of
his wife; he thought her the most beautiful and
most perfect woman who ever lived; and he
would not have been afraid to strike the king
himself, if he had gainsaid him on that point.
Still, there were those in the parish who were
of a different opinion; for rejected suitors are not
apt to make very warm friends afterwards, and
their mothers and sisters still less so. To Ingeborg it mattered little what people said; she carried her head as high after her wedding as she
had done in her maiden days, and shook hands
with the parishioners on Sundays after service
as friendly as ever. Then something happened
which made a change in her life.

Erick Skogstad had been one of Ingeborg's
warmest admirers. She had refused him twice,
but still he did not despair. He was present at

her wedding, and had been drunk even on the
second day. The sixth winter after, he invited
Sigurd and Ingeborg to his own wedding. They
both rode to church with the bridal party, but
Ingeborg excused · herself from coming in the
evening; she could not leave her baby, she said;
so Sigurd went alone. The second night more
than half of the guests were drunk, and even the
bridegroom himself had clearly looked " a little
too deep into the glass." Sigurd was displeased.
He left the hot, noisy hall, where the din was
almost deafening, and went out into the yard to
cool himself. The moon shone bright, and there
was a clear frost. He had meant to steal away
unnoticed, when the bridegroom and three or four
guests met him in the yard and stopped him.
" Where is your wife ? " asked Erick.

" She is at home."

" Why did n't she come ? Perhaps she thought
herself too good to come to Erick Skogstad's wedding."

" She could not leave her baby," replied Sigurd,
calmly, taking no notice of the latter remark.

"Could not leave her baby, hey?" cried Erick; "if she cannot leave her baby, then you may tell her from Erick Skogstad not to send her baby to a wedding alone another time." And seizing Sigurd with both hands by the coat-collar, he thrust his face close up to his and burst into a wild laughter.

"What do you mean?" said Sigurd, releasing himself from Erick's grasp.

"I mean that you are a baby, and that you had better go home and put on one of your wife's petticoats, and not come here and mingle with men." Erick was very much amused at his own taunts, and turned round to his attendants, laughing. They all laughed and looked scornfully at Sigurd. His arm trembled; he struggled hard to keep calm.

"You are afraid now, Sigurd Rimul," cried the bridegroom, again seizing him by the collar.

"Never shall you see the day when Sigurd Rimul is afraid." A heavy blow sent Erick headlong to the ground; for a moment he lay silent and moved not a finger; then with a fearful yell he bounded to his feet, lifted his huge fist, and rushed furiously against his opponent; but Sigurd was prepared, and warded off the blow with his arm. Erick foamed with rage; he felt for his knife, but fortunately it was gone, or that night might have been a bloody one. Then with both arms he caught his guest round the waist, and tried to throw him. The other struggled to free himself; but before he succeeded, Erick had tripped him, and his head struck heavily against the frozen ground, with Erick's large body upon it. Erick rose and looked at Sigurd: Sigurd did not rise.

It was about midnight. Ingeborg was sitting up with her sick child; she heard a noise in the hall, laid the child on the bed, and opened the door. Four men came into the room bearing something between them. They laid her husband upon the bed. "Almighty God, what have you done with him?" she shrieked.

"He quarrelled with Erick Skogstad and got the worst of it," said one of the men.

Sigurd was never himself again. The doctor

said that he had received a severe shock of the
brain. He was like a child, and hardly knew
anybody. A year after he died, and before long
the oldest child followed him.

Four winters had passed since Ingeborg buried
her husband; still she was the same stately woman to look at, and people saw little change in
her. Now she lived as a rich widow on a large
estate, and again people began to whisper of suitors and wooing. But they soon ceased, for the
widow of Rimul was not backward in showing the
lads in the valley that she had not changed her
mind since her maiden days.

Ragnhild Rimul, Ingeborg's daughter, was fairer
than spring. If Ingeborg's hair had been fair and
golden, her daughter's was fairer still; if Ingeborg's eyes had been deep and blue, Ragnhild's
were deeper and bluer. The young birch is light
and slender; and when by chance it grows alone
in the dark, heavy pine forest, it looks lighter and
more slender. Ragnhild was a birch in the pine
forest. Spring and sunshine were always about
her.

The sitting-room at Rimul was large and light. The windows looked east and south, and the floor was always strewn with fresh juniper-needles. In the corner between the windows was a little book-shelf with a heavy silver-clasped Bible, a few hymn-books, and a "house-postille," or a book of daily devotions. Under the book-shelf was what Ragnhild called her corner, where she had her little chair, and kept her shells, pieces of broken china, and other precious things. There was no stove in the room, but an open hearth, before which stood a large arm-chair, which in former times had belonged to Sigurd's father and grandfather, and had been standing there ever since. The room had a ceiling of unpainted planks, and the timber walls still retained the pleasant color of fresh-hewn pine beams. A door led from the sitting-room into the chamber where Ingeborg and her daughter slept. In another building across the yard were the barns, the stables, and the servant-hall. The maids slept in the cow-stable, which almost rivalled the dwelling-house in comfort and neatness. Behind the buildings the land rose more abruptly toward the mountains, but the slope was overgrown with thick-leaved groves, whose light foliage gradually shaded into the dark pine forest above. The fields of Rimul reached from the mansion down to where the river joined the fjord.

Sunshine had always been scarce there in the valley; Rimul, however, had the advantage of all other places, for the sun always came first there and lingered longest. Thus it had sun both within and without.

IV.

LAYS AND LEGENDS.

LD GUNHILD had been a good singer in her time; indeed, she had quite a fine voice even now, perhaps a little husky at times and rather low for a woman. But Thor and Gunnar, at least, both thought it wonderfully melodious, and there is no doubt but it was remarkably well adapted to the wild and doleful lays it was her wont to sing.

One winter night the fire burnt cheerfully on the hearth, and they were all gathered round it as usual; Thor smoking, and working at his spoons and boxes, Gunnar eagerly listening to his grandmother's stories.

"Sing, now, grandmother," demanded the boy, as a marvellous Trold-story had just been finished.

"Very well. What do you want?" For grandmother was always ready to sing.

"Something about the Hulder." And she sang
of a young man who lay down in the woods to
sleep, but could not sleep for the strange voices
he heard from flower and river and mountain ;
then over them all stole the sad, joyful, yearning
tones of the Hulder's loor; and anon he beheld
a beautiful maiden in scarlet bodice and golden
hair, who fled before him night and day through
the forest, till he heard the sound of the Sabbath-
bell. He whispered the name of Christ : —

> " Then saw I the form of the maiden fair
> Vanish as mist in the morning air.

> " With the last toll of the Sabbath-bell
> Gone was the maiden and broken the spell.

> " O young lads and maidens, beware, beware,
> In the darksome woods,
> The treacherous Hulder is playing there
> In the darksome woods."

After running through some wild mournful
notes, Gunhild's voice gradually sank into a low,
inarticulate murmur. Thor's box was no nearer

3   D

done than when the song commenced, and his pipe had gone out. Gunnar's eyes rested dreamily in the fire. For a while they all sat in silence. Gunhild was the first to speak.

"What are you staring at, child?" said she.

Gunnar did not hear.

"What are you looking for in the fire, child?" repeated the grandmother a little louder. Gunnar seemed to wake up as from some beautiful dream, which he tried to keep, but could not.

"Why, grandmother, what did you do that for?" said he, slowly and reluctantly turning his eyes from the flickering flames.

"Do what, child?" asked his grandmother, half frightened at the strange look in his eyes.

"You scared her away," said he, gloomily.

"Scared whom away?"

"The Hulder with scarlet bodice and golden hair."

"Bless you, child! Whatever you do, don't look at me in that way. Come, let the Hulder alone, and let us talk about something else."

"Another story?"

"As you please, another story."

But Gunhild knew very little about other things than Necks, Hulders, and fairies, and before long she was deep in another legend of the same nature. This was what she told : —

"He who is sorrowful knows Necken, and Necken knows him best who is sorrowful. When the heart is light, the ear is dull; but when the eye is dimmed by the hidden tear, then the soul is in the ear, and it can hear voices in the forest and sea which are dumb to the light-hearted. I remember the day when old Gunnar first told me that I was fair, and said his heart and his cottage would always have a place for me. I was gay and happy then; my heart danced in my bosom, and my feet beat the time on the ground. I went to the old cataract. It cared little for my joy; it looked cold and dreary.

"Two years from that day the church-bells tolled over my first-born. My heart was heavy, and my eye so hot that it burned the tear before it could reach the eyelid. Again I sat on Necken's stone at the cataract, and from the waters arose

strange music, sad but sweet and healing, like
the mild shower after the scorching heat. Then
the tears started and I wept, and the music wept
too; we wept together, and neither of us knew
who stopped first. Since then I have always loved
the old cataract; for now I know that it is true,
as the legend says, that Necken plays his harp
there amid the roar of the waters. And Necken
knows sorrow; he loved, but he loved in vain.

"Love is like fire, child; love is like fire.
Wounds of fire are hard to heal; harder still are
those of love. Necken loved a mortal maiden;
fair was she like the morning, but fickle as the
sea-wind. It was a midsummer morning he saw
her last, and midsummer night she had promised
to wed him. Midsummer night came, but she
came not. It is said to be years and years ago;
but still the midsummer night has never missed
him, as he raises his head above the water, looking for his bride, when the midnight hour strikes.
Strangely, then, do the mournful chords tremble
through the forests in the lonely night; for he
calls his bride. If they ever reached her ear, no

one knows; but that lad or that maiden who
comes to the cataract at the midnight hour will
hear the luring music, and he who loves in truth
and loves in sorrow will never go away uncom-
forted. Many a fair maiden has spoken there the
desire of her heart, and has been heard; many a
rejected wooer came there with a heart throbbing
with love and heavy with sorrow; he has called
for help and help he has found, if he was worthy
thereof. For Necken knows the heart of man;
he rewards him who is worthy of reward, and
punishes him who deserves punishment. Many a
lad wooes a maiden, but loves her gold. Such also
have sought the cataract at the midnight hour;
they have never since been seen, for they never
returned. An invisible arm has hurled them down
into the whirling pools, and their cries have been
heard from afar, as they were seized by the seeth-
ing rapids.

"Long ago, when my forehead was smooth like
the fjord in the summer morning, when my cheek
was as fresh as the early dawn, and my hair like
a wheat-field in September, then I knew a lad

whom no one will forget who had ever seen him; and that lad was Saemund of Fagerlien. Never eagle, however high its flight, was safe from his arrow; never bear made his den too deep for him to find it; never a beam was built beyond the reach of his heel.

"Saemund's father was a houseman; had no farm for his son, no silver spoons or costly linen. But if you wanted to see sport, you ought to have gone to the dance when Saemund was there. Never that girl lived, gardman's or houseman's daughter, who did not feel her heart leap in her bosom when he offered to lead her in the lusty spring-dance. He never challenged a man to fight, but too late that man repented who offered him a challenge.

"The sun shone on many fair maidens in those days; but strength is failing now, and beauty is fading, and the maidens nowadays are not like those who lived before them. But even then no lad who had cast his eyes on Margit of Elgerfold would wish to look at another maiden. For when she was present, all others faded, like a cluster of pines when a white birch sprouts in the midst of them. Thorkild of Elgerfold was at that time surely the proudest, and, likely enough, also among the richest in the parish. He had no other child than Margit, and there was no lad in the valley he thought good enough for her.

" I have often heard old and truthful people say, that there were more wooers in one week at Elger-fold in those days than all the other maidens of the valley saw all the year round. Old Thorkild, Margit's father, did not fancy that wooing-busi-ness ; but Margit had always been used to have her own way ; so it was just as well to say noth-ing about it.

" Then came winter, and with winter came gay feasts, weddings, and merry dancing-parties. Of course Margit was there, and as for Saemund, no wedding or party was complete without him ; they might as well have failed to ask the bridegroom. But people would say, that during that winter he led Margit of Elgerfold in the dance perhaps a little oftener than was agreeable to old Thorkild, her father. He was only a houseman's son, you know, and she was a rich man's daughter. And if you did not try to shut your eyes, you could not help noticing that Margit's sparkling eyes never shone as brightly as when Saemund asked her to dance, and the smile on her lips never was sweeter and happier than when she rested on his arm.

"When winter was over, Margit went to the saeter * with the cattle; the saeter-road was quite fashionable that summer; probably it was more frequented than even the highway. And a gay time they had up there, for there was hardly a lad, gardman's or houseman's son, who did not visit the saeter of Elgerford; and especially on Saturday eves, scores of young men would chance to meet on the saeter-green. The girls from the neighboring sacters would be sent for, and the night would be sure to end with a whirling spring-dance. But one was missed in the

* Saeter is a place in the mountains where the Norwegian peasants spend their summers, pasturing their cattle. In the interior districts the whole family generally goes to the saeter, while in the lower valleys they send only their daughters and one or more maid-servants.

number of Margit's visitors, and that happened to
be he who would have been most welcome. Saemund had shouldered his gun and spent the long
summer days hunting. He had never been at the
saeter of Elgerfold; and as there were no parties
at that season, he and Margit hardly ever saw
each other.

"People were busy talking at that time, as
people always are. Why did Margit, said they,
before summer was over, dismiss every one of her
suitors, even the sons of the mightiest men in the
parish? Of course, because she had taken it into
her foolish head that she wanted somebody
who did not want her, and the only one who
did not seem to want her was Saemund of
Fagerlien. Now parish talk is not altogether to ·
be trusted, but neither is it altogether to be dis-
believed; for there always is some truth at the
bottom, and the end showed that this was not
gathered altogether from the air * either, as the

---

* A common expression in Norway for something that
seems to have originated without any apparent cause or foundation.

saying is. Margit had gold, and she had beauty; but for all that she was but a weak woman, and what woman's heart could resist those bottomless eyes of Saemund's? Surely, Margit had soon found that she could not. So she thought the matter over, until at last she discovered that there was hardly one thought in her soul which was not already his. But what should she do? 'Here at home he will never come to see me,' said she to herself, 'for he knows father would not like it. I had better go to the saeter, and have the boys come to visit me there; then, when all the rest go, he will hardly be the only one to stay away.' But summer came and went, and saeter-time was nearly gone. Yet he had not come. 'This will not do,' thought Margit; 'perhaps he imagines I intend to marry some one of the gardmans' lads, since they come here so often.' And she dismissed them all. Now he must surely come. But autumn came, and the fall storms, the messengers of winter, swept through the valley and stripped the forest of its beauty. Yet he had not come. It was cold on

the saeter then, and thick clouds in the east fore-
boded snow. .Then old Thorkild himself went to
the saeter, and wanted to know why his daughter
had not come home with the cattle long ago.
It certainly was madness to stay in the mountains
now, so late in the season, when the hoar-frost
covered the fields and the pasture was nearly
frozen. Perhaps the hoar-frost had touched Margit's cheeks, too, for the spring-like roses were
fading fast, and the paleness of winter was taking
their place. 'She has caught a bad cold,' said
her father; 'she stayed too late in the mountains.'

"People seldom saw Saemund that summer.
All they knew was that he was in the highlands
hunting. Now and then he would appear in the
valley at the office of the judge with two or three
bear-skins, and receive his premiums. Nobody
could understand why he did not go to the Elgerfold saeter, like all the other lads; for there was
no doubt he would be welcome. But Saemund
himself well knew why he stayed away. If he
had not felt that Margit of Elgerfold was dearer

to him than he even liked to own to himself, he might perhaps have seen her oftener. It is only a foolish fancy, thought he, at first; when summer comes it will pass away. But summer came, and Saemund found that his foolish fancy was getting the better of him. He did not know what to make of himself. How could he, a low-born houseman's son, have the boldness to love the fairest and richest heiress in all the valley? How could he ever expect to marry her? The thought was enough to drive him mad.

"Winter came, and Margit was waiting still. Winter went; Saemund had not yet come. Spring dawned, the forest was budding, and midsummer drew near.

"'There is no other way,' thought Margit, as she sat in her garret-window and saw the silence of the midsummer night stealing over the fjord, the river, and the distant forests. Even the roaring of the cataract sounded half smothered and faint. 'There is no other way,' repeated she. 'I will try, and if I am wrong — well, if I am wrong, then may God be merciful to me.' She went to the door of her father's room and listened; he slept. She wavered no longer. The cataract was not far away; soon she was there. The doleful cry of an owl was the first sound to break the silence; she stopped and shuddered, for the owl is a prophet of evil. Then an anxious hush stole through the forest, and in another moment the silence was breathless; Margit listened; she heard but the beating of her own heart, then something like a strange whispering hum below, overhead, and all around her. She felt that it was the midnight hour coming. It seemed to her that she was moving, but she knew not whither her feet carried her. When her sight cleared, she found herself at the edge of the cataract. There she knelt down.

" ' Neckcn,' prayed she, ' hear me, O hear me ! Margit's heart is full of sorrow, and none but thou canst help her. Long has she loved Saemund, long has she waited, but he would not come.' ' Margit, he has come,' whispered a well-known voice in her ear, and Margit sank in Saemund's arms. Long had she waited, at last he had come;

and as their hearts and their lips met, they heard
and they felt the sounds of wonderful harmony.
It was the tones of Necken's harp. Both had
sought and both had found him."

V.

EARLY EXPERIENCES.

GUNNAR did not like spelling half as well as his grandmother's stories, and Gunhild had to use all her powers of persuasion before she could convince him of the necessity of learning the alphabet. He soon, however, learned to know the letters and to draw them on the floor, with beards, tails, and other fanciful additions. He had an original way of attributing certain good or bad traits of character to each letter of the alphabet, and of showing a decided favor for some in preference to others. He could well understand why "Hulder" should commence with "H,"* he said, for the H was always, like the Hulder, trying to

---

* H in the German, not in the English, alphabet. The German alphabet is mostly used in Norway.

curl up its tail to keep it out of sight. But in spite of all difficulties, and in spite of all the ill-treatment of the Catechism, which had to serve both as spelling-book and for religious instruction, Gunhild did not give up; and after two years of persevering toil, she at last had the satisfaction of knowing that her pupil had read the book five times through, and could say the Lord's Prayer and Apostles' Creed both forwards and backwards.

Thor did not think it well for the boy to stay at home any longer with his grandmother; he knew already too much about Hulders, Trolds, and fairies, and he could hardly open his mouth about anything else. He was old enough now to be of some use, and as soon as he could find any one who wanted him he would send him away. Gunhild protested, but it was in vain : his mother might have known that; for Thor never changed his mind.

One night he came home and told her that he had made arrangements with the widow of Rimul, who wanted Gunnar to watch her cattle in the mountains through the summer; the boy would have to be ready to start for the saeter at daybreak the next morning. Gunnar's heart beat loud for joy when he heard this; he had nearly laughed right out, and would have done so, if he had not been afraid of offending his grandmother.

Next morning all rose with the sun. They ate their breakfast in silence. When the heart is full, it is hard to speak. When they were about to start, the grandmother gave Gunnar a small bundle, with a hymn-book, a coat, and a shirt for change.

"The coat you must only wear on Sundays," said she, the tears nearly choking her voice. "When you hear the church-bells chime from the valley, then you must read a hymn and the gospel for the day in the back part of the book; then nothing evil can befall thee. On week-days you must always go in your shirt-sleeves, except when it is very cold." The last advice Gunnar hardly heard, he was so anxious to be off.

Father and son walked rapidly down towards

E

the boat-house. It was early in June. The sun shone brightly, and the morning fog was slowly rising from the fields and from the river. Gunnar could not help turning his head often to look from a distance at the old cottage which he had now quitted for the first time in his life; and as long as the turf-covered roof was in sight, he could see his grandmother standing in the door, wiping the tears from her eyes with her apron. Gunnar for a moment was quite touched; he felt the tears starting, and it suddenly occurred to him that he surely loved his grandmother very much.

When they reached Atle Henjum's boat-house, Thor untied a boat, and they crossed the river. Rimul lay on the hillside, smiling in the morning sun. The fjord looked as if it wanted to speak, but was too happy to find expression; therefore it remained silent, but gazed at the wanderers with those strange speaking though speechless eyes, which no one ever forgets who has ever penetrated to the heart of Norway.

There was a great noise and bustle at Rimul.

Everybody, from the mistress to the house-cat, seemed to be too busy to take any notice of Thor and Gunnar, as they passed through the gate into the yard. The boys were loading the backs of the horses with buckets, kettles, blankets, and all kinds of household utensils; while the girls were marking the ears of the sheep and goats, and tying bells round the necks of the most distinguished members of the flock. On a sloping bridge, leading from the yard into the upper floor of the barn, stood a tall, fair woman, with a large white cloth tied in a peculiar fashion around her head. It was bound tightly round the forehead, but widened behind into the shape of a semicircle. The fair woman seemed so absorbed in the orders she was giving in a loud voice to different parties working in the yard, that she did not observe Thor, before he was right at her side.

"Thanks for the last meeting," said Thor, taking off his cap and extending his hand.

"Thanks to yourself, Thor," said Ingeborg of Rimul; for it was she to whom Thor had addressed his words.

"It will be a warm day," observed Thor.

"Therefore we want to get the cattle off at once; if we tarry, they will scatter before noon and we shall not know where to look for them. Glad you came so early, Thor. Is this your boy?"

Gunnar had sought refuge behind his father.

"This is my boy. Go and shake hands, Gunnar."

The boy obeyed, though rather reluctantly.

"Gunnar; a good old name. How old are you, Gunnar?"

"Don't know," said Gunnar.

"Eleven years last Christmas," replied his father.

"That little girl you see down there among the sheep," continued Ingeborg, still addressing the boy, "is Gudrun Henjum, my brother's daughter. Go and speak to her. I have something to say to your father."

There was something severe in the woman's way of talking, and he felt rather inclined to rebel. How could he go and speak to a little

girl, — he who had hardly ever seen a little girl
before? What should he speak to her about?
Thus pondering, he had nearly reached the foot
of the bridge, when a sudden powerful thrust
from behind sent him headlong down into the
yard. He was so surprised that he hardly knew
whether to laugh or to cry. As he was trying to
get on his feet again, he discovered a large ram
standing a few yards from him, evidently prepar-
ing for another attack. A merry ringing laugh
caught his ear, and as he looked up he saw two
little girls coming to his rescue. That was more
than he could bear. In a moment, springing to
his feet, he seized the ram by the horns, and shook
him with all his might.

"Why, you naughty boy!" cried one of the
girls, "you must not treat Hans so badly. Don't
you understand, he only wants to play with you."
Gunnar felt rebuked. He released the ram, and
for a while stood gazing at the little girl and the
little girl stood gazing at him, each of them expecting the other to speak first. The little girl
had a scarlet bodice and golden hair.

" Are you the Hulder ? " said he at last, in order to say something.

" Mother, mother," cried she, running up to where Thor and Ingeborg were standing, " what do you think he is saying ? He wants to know if I am the Hulder."

" Be quiet, child," said Ingeborg, sternly, " I have no time to speak to you."

Abashed at the rebuke, the little girl turned slowly, twisted the corner of her apron between her fingers with an expression of embarrassment, and after some hesitation again returned to Gunnar.

" Have you got a name ? " asked she.

" Yes," answered he.

" My name is Ragnhild, and this is Gudrun, my cousin."

Here she pointed to another little girl, who seemed to be of about the same age as herself; in other respects there was but little resemblance. Gudrun was not so fair, and had a certain look of shyness about her.

" My name is Gunnar; and grandmother knows

a great many stories about Necken and the Hulder, and the boy who killed the Trold and married
the beautiful princess."

The girls were astounded at such wisdom.

" Who is Necken ? " asked Ragnhild.

" Why, don't you know about Necken ? he who
plays every midsummer night in the water under
the great waterfall yonder ? "

" Plays in the water ? Who told you ? " And
a shade of doubt passed over Ragnhild's expressive
features.

" Well, if you don't believe it, you may ask
grandmother ; she knows."

" Who is grandmother ? "

" Why, my grandmother of course."

Here the conversation was interrupted by the
coming of Thor and Ingeborg.

The long, clear tones of the loor streamed
through the valley and resounded between the
mountains. It was the signal that the caravan
was starting. Suddenly all was life and motion
throughout the wide yard. The call of the loor
seemed to impart joy and animation to everything

it reached. The cattle bellowed, the calves and
the goats danced, the milkmaids sung, and the
forest far and near echoed with joyous song and
clamor. From her elevated station on the bridge
of the barn, Ingeborg still continued issuing her
final orders with regard to the order of the march,
until the back gate of the yard was opened and
the lads led the loaded pack-horses up along a
steep and stony road, which climbed over the
wood-clothed mountain-side and gradually lost itself in the thicket ; after the horses followed Thor
and Gunnar with the goats and sheep ; and last
came the girls, driving before them the herd of
larger cattle. All the girls and most of the men
had long loors in their hands ; and high above the
noise of the lowing cattle and the merry chat and
laughter of the girls flowed the loor-tones from
mountain to mountain, like an eagle soaring
over all the littleness of the world below. The
cattle knew the loor, and followed it instinctively :
it is the surest messenger of spring, and as such is
as welcome as the lark and swallow.

The loor is the song of the dark Norwegian pine

forest; it is the voice of Norway's cloud-hooded mountain; it has a traditional history as old and as romantic as that of the troubadour's guitar in the Middle Ages; and surely no Spanish donna or Italian signora ever listened more expectantly to the music of a nightly serenade than the simple saeter-maid when the echo of the loor tells her that her lover is on his way from the valley. This has always been his greeting; and she takes her own loor, puts it to her mouth, and the mountains far and near resound with her welcome.

Soon the last calf has left the yard. Ingeborg of Rimul is still standing on the same spot, viewing with apparent pleasure, and not without a certain pride, the long caravan, as it slowly winds along the steep saeter-road. And, in truth, it is a beautiful sight: the men in their light, close-fitting knee-breeches, scarlet vests, and little, red, pointed caps; the girls with their long blond hair flowing down over their shoulders, their white linen sleeves, and bright bodices; the varied colors of the cattle all standing in fine relief against

4

the dark hue of the forest, which on both sides encloses the road. When the caravan was out of sight, Ingeborg rose, with a contented smile.

"I should like to see the man," said she to herself, "who has finer flocks on this side the mountains."

Thor and his son walked in silence up the steep mountain path, driving the goats before them. Gunnar was looking eagerly for the Hulder, whose scarlet bodice he expected to discover at every bend of the path. All his looking was vain; but although greatly disappointed, he felt by no means inclined to give up. At noon they had walked about eight miles without resting. Then the view, which had hitherto been shut in on all sides by the thick-growing pine-trunks, suddenly opened upon a wide, glittering lake, whose water was so clear that they could hardly decide where it touched the air; for the bottom was visible as far as the eye could reach. Gunnar gave a cry of delight at the sight of the lake: he had never seen a lake before. Here men and cattle halted to take their noon rest. He in the mean time climbed up

on a rock projecting far into the water, and sat
there watching the fishes chasing each other
round, and playing hide-and-seek between the
stones and rushes down on the bottom

In about an hour the loor again sounded, and
the party again broke up. The farther they went,
the steeper became the road; and gradually, as
they ascended, the forest grew thinner, and the
whole landscape assumed a wilder and sterner
character. Instead of the slender, stately pine,
the crippled dwarf birch was seen creeping along
the stony ground; everything was so barren, so
lifeless; and the barrenness of the monotonous
scenery seemed to impress both men and cattle.
The song and the laughter ceased, and the bells
of the cows were the only sound to break the silence.

It was already late in the afternoon. The landscape still wore the same unseemly garb of dust-
brown heather, interwoven with the twisted and
knotted stems of the dwarf birch, running length-
wise and crosswise in every possible direction, and
with their coarse, mazy network binding the in-

coherent elements of the landscape together. Suddenly came a loud shout from the foremost man.

" The highland, the highland ! " ran from mouth to mouth ; and, joining in the joyful cry, girls and men, hurrying the cattle onward, bounded from stone to stone as fast as their feet could carry them. At the border of the wide highland plain they all halted : one powerful tone from thirty united loors rolled over the crowns of the mountains ; it was their greeting to the highland. Numerous flocks of screaming birds flew up from the plain in answer to the greeting.

Gunnar was among the last comers. To him, who had no idea of what a highland meant, and who never had been used to see more than a few rods around him, the change was so sudden and so unexpected that for a moment he had a sensation as if he was losing his breath, or as if the earth had fallen from under his feet, and he had been left floating in the air. The next sensation was one of blindness ; for the immense distance dazzled his unwonted eye almost as if he had been gazing at the sun. Speechless he stared before him. Gradually the objects which had at first appeared near together separated, and the vast table-land spread before him in all its unlimited grandeur. He drew a long, full breath : surely he had never known the delight of breathing before. A throng of childish plans crowded into his mind ; half-hidden dreams, half-born hopes, revived, and came forth into light : they had not had room while they were crowded together down in the dark, narrow valley.

Gunnar felt strong and free. He sat down on the soft verdure, and drank new delight from the glorious sight. The whole plain was overgrown with rich, fresh, green grass. A few miles away lay a large mountain lake ; and a clear, broad river wound quietly through the imposing plateau. On a slight elevation near the lake-shore lay three turf-thatched chalets, hedged in by a fence of low palisades ; that was the saeter of Rimul. In the blue distance a Yokul lifted its airy head into the clouds. Suddenly his grandmother's old, forbidden story of the poor boy, the three-headed Trold, and the beautiful princess, stood vividly before Gunnar's mind. When the poor boy had walked a long way and had reached the top of the first mountain, he had met an old woman, of whom he had asked the way. "Can you see that high mountain, far away in the blue distance?" the old woman asked.

Yes, the boy could see that mountain.

"Well," continued the old woman, "ten thousand miles beyond it is another far higher mountain. There is the palace of the Trold; there sleeps the beautiful princess."

"This must surely be the right mountain," thought Gunnar. "O, could I but see beyond it!"

Before long the caravan was again moving, and he was no longer left to his own meditations. Indeed, the goats gave him enough to do for the remainder of the day, and he soon had a foretaste of the unpleasant part of the duties of a "cattle-boy." The goats did not seem at all disposed to keep company; and when that animal has formed a determination, it is not easily prevailed against

either by force or by cunning. But in spite of
the resolute resistance on the part of the goats,
Gunnar at last had the triumph of seeing his
rebellious subjects gathered with the rest of the
party on the saeter-green. The saeter cottages
were opened, and the horses unloaded. Before
the door of the middle cottage, out in the open
air, there was a large fireplace built of rough
stones; here a fire was made, and the wooden
cups and milk-pails were boiled with juniper
branches, before they were taken into use; for
unless thus prepared they would give a wooden
taste to the milk.

It was indeed a welcome sight to Gunnar when
at length a repast, consisting of oatmeal and dried
beef, was spread on the grass; and he was certainly not the only one who looked forward with
eagerness to the approaching feast. All preparations being finished, the merry company sat down
round the fire, and attacked the solid food with an
enviable appetite.

When the meal was at an end, it was already
late in the afternoon. The cattle would find pas-

ture within the corral that night, and the hour for milking was near. The maids then went to their work, and the men to theirs.

"Poor lads we have nowadays," said Brita, a tall, slender girl, with a mass of rich blond hair flowing down over her back, and deep dimples in her cheeks, — "poor lads we have nowadays! Among so many, not one who knows how to tread the spring-dance decently." And she put down the filled milk-pails she was carrying, set her arms akimbo, and, with an air of roguish defiance, fixed her eyes upon a group of young men who lay lazily smoking around the fire.

"Did you ever hear of the chicken who wanted to teach the hen to lay eggs?" answered a young lad in the smoking group, to whom the challenge seemed to be especially addressed.

"The best buck is not always the one that has the biggest horns, Endre," laughed the girl. "Your strength has always been in the mouth, you know; your legs are certainly more than long enough, if you only knew how to use them."

"Canute, halloo! Out with the fiddle," cried Endre to an older man, who was sitting on the threshold of the cottage leisurely smoking his evening pipe, — "out with the fiddle, I say! and Brita shall soon see whether I understand how to use my legs or not."

Canute soon got his eight-stringed Hardanger violin in order, struck a few strangely sounding chords by way of prelude, and began. Brita was only too glad to accept Endre's invitation. The other young men follow his example; and before long the whole crowd is moving in a ring around the fire in time with the alluring music. Only Thor does not dance; he takes a seat at the fiddler's side, and soon seems entirely absorbed in the contemplation of the smoke from his pipe, as it curls up, spreads, and slowly vanishes in the clear night-air. Probably he is musing over the days when he ranked the foremost among the dancers of the valley. Gunnar looks in wonder at this unwonted sight; and the longer he listens to the exciting notes the stronger a desire he feels to join. Now the music comes softly rippling

4*   F

from the strings, now it rolls and rumbles, and now again flows smooth and clear, until it hushes itself into a gentle, whispering murmur. And the dancers understand and they feel the power of that music. First forming a long line, they move slowly forward, leading the girls by the hands after them, and softly touching the ground alternately with their heels and toes, and adapting the gestures of their whole bodies to the rippling tones; but gradually, as the strokes of the fiddler grow wilder, the tread of their heels becomes stronger, and the motions of their limbs more wildly expressive.

It was late, but still the sun was lingering; it looked red and tired, for it had waked many hours. One long, loving, parting look, and it sunk in a dreamy halo behind the western glaciers. A nightly chill crept over the highland.

The dance was ended. Canute, the fiddler, carefully wrapped his precious violin in his handkerchief to protect it from the damp night-air. Gunnar, who had looked on and listened until he was fast asleep, was aroused by his father. " I am going home again now," said Thor, "but I shall come up here to see you now and then. Here, take this as a keepsake from your father." And Thor went. Gunnar had hardly time to realize whether he was awake or dreaming. It was a fine knife, with carved haft and silver sheath, he held in his hand. He had long wished for just such a knife. Surely he had never known his father before now. He saw that clearly.

VI.

RHYME-OLA.

GUNNAR sat on the lake-shore musing; he stared down into the deep, clear water. The sun stood right in the north. Round about lay the cattle in their noon rest. Although it was but three weeks to-day since he had come to the saeter, it was to him an infinitely long time; he appeared to himself so much older and wiser; and the little boy who a few weeks ago rode on Fox and talked to the dark was as far off as if he had but heard of him in some Neck or Hulder legend. And the poor boy who slew the Trold and married the princess! curious it would be to know if he had ever been in the highlands and watched cattle.

How strange it looked down there in the water! How wonderfully cool and clear! Now a big, shining dragon-fly came dancing away over the invisible mirror, gently touched it, and small, quivering rings spread and spread, and vanished, — vanished somewhere and nowhere. How wonderfully still! The water rested, the air rested, everything rested. No sound, no motion. But the silence seemed to make everything look stronger, to color and intensify it. Down there on the bottom of the lake the gray stones lay between the tall, rustling bulrushes; and they grew and moved, drew nearer and nearer. Gunnar, half frightened, turned his eyes swiftly, flung himself on his back, and gazed up into the air. There was not a cloud to be seen; the air was a great nothing. And the longer he gazed the weaker he appeared to himself, as if he was losing himself in the clearness of the air; and the air grew stronger and stronger; it began to float and move before his eyes, until at last an infinite number of small colorless disks came slowly swimming past him, and filled the space far and near. Then by degrees they assumed a faint violet or blue color, faded, and again grew brighter. A flash of light from nowhere and everywhere leaped through the air, trembled, glittered, and vanished. And the air itself vanished too. Again it was as nothing. He shut his eyes. How strange!

Then it was as if something spoke, — spoke without a sound, yet distinctly and audibly; without word, yet full of hidden meaning. He listened; and the longer he listened the dimmer grew the boundary between silence and sound, until they strangely blended. The silence seemed the symphony of an infinite number of infinitely small voices too small to be called sounds; they gushed forth all round him and from within him; they whizzed in the air, they buzzed in the grass, the bulrushes rustled with them. Suddenly, as he became conscious that he was listening, the sound stopped, as in wonder at its own existence, and a vast emptiness filled the world far and near. He held his breath; and as his thought lost its hold on itself, the air, the grass, the rushes, were again alive with numberless voices; but to him it seemed as if they had been forever, as if they had never suffered an interruption; for there was

that in their nature which has no beginning, neither has it any end. And as he lay there listening in half-conscious unconsciousness, the thought
shot through his mind that he must have seen
and heard all this before, he knew not when or
where. Then came the poor boy with his princess ; certainly, from his grandmother's tales, it
was there ; he knew it all. He felt as if he stood
at the entrance of that new world which, though
unknown and unseen, he had been vaguely conscious of through so many long years of yearning,
whose nearness he had felt many a dark winter
night when, after the tale was ended, the drowsy
embers from the hearth had stared at him with
weird, beckoning eyes ; when on Fox, the old saddle, he had ridden out in search of Trold, and
wonders ; when, up under the roof of the cottage,
he had spent such happy hours gazing at the
dark, and with the fantastic shapes of the dark
gazing at him. As all these impressions now
again stood vividly before him, he saw that they
had all been tones in the same chord. This was
the full chord ; still there was no rest in it, — it

was a chord of transition, a step to something higher. And the Hulder, — he felt her presence; she could not be far from him now.

A thundering noise struck his ear; he started to his feet, still dreaming, senseless, bewildered. He had half expected to see the golden hair and the scarlet bodice of the Hulder, and in the first moment he was not sure but it might be she. But before his second thought, he felt himself seized by the arm and flung up the hillside, and he thought he heard these words: "Whatever you do, boy, don't you rush right into the water!"

Gunnar rubbed his eyes and stared. He saw a queer-looking little man standing on the hillside, holding a long loor in his hand, and with a broad grin on his face.

"I do not think you are a very good cattle-boy," continued the man. "What do you think the widow of Rimul would say if she knew you went to sleep at this time of the day, and that right in the sunshine? If it had not been for me, you might have looked in the moon for your cows to-night. They were all straggling."

" I was not asleep," said Gunnar, now somewhat recovered.

He thought the little man was very queer-looking indeed. He was rather homely, some would, perhaps, say even ugly. His eyes were large and dark, and looked as if he had just been weeping; his mouth was broad, and drawn up to one side in a strange, half-sarcastic smile. There was an inexplicable conflict between the dreaming sadness of his eyes and the broad burlesque expression of the rest of his features. He seemed to be conscious of this himself; for he kept winking with one eye, as if trying to make this discordant feature conform to the leading characteristic of his face.

The little man flung himself down on the greensward and fixed his eyes intently on Gunnar; and the boy followed his example, and stared at him in return. Thus they sat for a while. At last the stranger opened his mouth as if he were going to speak, then shut it again without saying anything, and so again and again.

" Have you got anything to eat ?" cried he, suddenly, as if it cost him a great effort to speak the words.   .

" No," said Gunnar.

"Then come here," continued the other, "and hold this cow by the horns, while I milk her. I am hungry as a wolf."

Gunnar obeyed. There was something very peculiar in the little man, some strange mixture of strength and weakness, which did not fail to make a strong impression on his mind. While he held the cow, his companion stooped down, milked with one hand, using the other for a cup, and now and then emptying it into his mouth. But after a while, probably finding this process too trouble-some, he knelt down, put his head up under the cow, and milked right into his mouth.

"Does the cow kick?" asked he.

"Yes."

"Very well." And he went on milking, while Gunnar stood gazing at him in mute astonish-ment. At last the cow began to show signs of impatience.

"Ah," said he, rising, and wiping the milk from

his mouth with his ragged coat-sleeve, "what a delicious meal! I have not seen a thing to eat since yesterday noon; and since this morning my miserable bowels have been entertaining me with a wofuller Lenten-hymn than ever found its way into old Kingo's hymn-book. Strange enough, I never was partial to fasting."

And he laughed aloud; but finding no response in Gunnar, whose face was as grave as ever, he suddenly stayed his mirth, and with a look of disappointment turned on his heel and seated himself in the grass, with his back to his companion. Gunnar, however, unconscious of offence, walked up to him, and flung himself down at his side on the green. The man then, after having examined all his pockets, finally from the one on the inside of his vest drew out some ragged and greasy papers, which he carefully spread out on his knees, and for some time contemplated, with an expression of the keenest interest. Soon his mouth was again drawn up into its customary grin or smile, and his face grew brighter and happier the longer he looked. Gunnar was quite curious to know what these old papers could contain; for, judging from the expression of the man's face, they surely afforded him great delight. Now he shook his head and laughed heartily. The boy could no longer restrain his curiosity.

"What is your name?" asked he, rather abruptly.

The man was so absorbed in his papers that he heard nothing.

"What is your name?" repeated Gunnar, this time close to his ear.

The little man quickly raised his head, and looked round bewildered, as if he had been suddenly awaked from some delightful revery.

"My name?" said he; "my name? Sure enough; that is more easily asked than told. I have such a great number of names, that I hardly think I can remember them all."

"Then tell me only one of them."

"Well, if you are so very anxious to know, I will tell you as many as you can bear to hear. Some call me Fool-Ola, others Rag-Ola; but with the pastor and all the gentlefolk of the valley I generally go by the name of Rhyme-Ola."

"Why, indeed! Are you Rhyme-Ola?"

"They say so."

"I have heard grandmother speak of you. She knows a great many of your songs too." Rhyme-Ola's sad eyes brightened, but he said nothing. Gunnar was very anxious to know something about the papers, but he hardly knew how to approach the subject. At last he made an attempt. "Is there anything written in those papers of yours?" asked he.

"Written!" cried Rhyme-Ola, in sudden excitement; "written, did you say? No, sir; there is nothing written on my papers, — nothing *written*," with an indignant emphasis on the last word.

"I beg your pardon. I did not know there was any harm in asking," said Gunnar, quite frightened by the irritation of his friend.

"No, sir; there is nothing *written*," repeated Rhyme-Ola, indignantly; "the pastor himself said that it was printed, — printed in the great city beyond the mountains, and read by all the judges and pastors all over the country. Then it cannot be written."

Upon Gunnar's further inquiry, Rhyme-Ola related with great minuteness a long story, of how he had once, a long time ago, sung one of his ditties to the old pastor, who was now dead and buried; how the old pastor had praised his song, and asked his permission to write it down, and send it to one of the city papers.

"That is a good song, Rhyme-Ola," the old pastor had said, "and worthy to live a long time after both you and I are dead and gone." So he had it sent to be printed in print, and these were the leaves on which the song had been printed. Never author found more happiness in his far-famed volume than this poor country songster in the long-forgotten newspaper in which his only song was printed. "It is to live after I am dead," muttered he, gazing at the half-worn-out leaves with eyes as tender as those of a mother looking on her first-born child.

Gunnar fully shared his delight, and looked upon the remnants of the song with reverence, as if they contained a world of wisdom.

"Could you not read the song for me?" asked he, eagerly.

"Read? I cannot read."

"Sing, then!"

"Yes, gladly will I sing." And Rhyme-Ola once more took his papers, turned, and examined them closely, running down the page with his finger, as if reading; at about the middle of the page he pointed at a line and called Gunnar. "Read there," said he: "what does it say?"

The paper was so soiled that Gunnar had great difficulty in making out what it was.

"Now, what does it say?" repeated the author, impatiently.

"The Bruised Wing: by Rhyme-Ola."

"By Rhyme-Ola; yes, that is right, by Rhyme-Ola." And he rose to his feet and sang:—

> " Little sparrow he sits on his roof so low,
>   Chirping the summer-day long.
>   The swallow she bathes in the sunlight's glow,
>   And lifts to the heavens her song.
>   But high is the flight of the eagle.
>
> " Little sparrow he buildeth his lowly nest
>   Close decked by the shingles red.
>   The swallow she findeth a better rest,

With her wings to the storm-wind wed.
And high is the flight of the eagle.

"The swallow she cometh from far away, .
O'er wild waves and mountains high ;
She comes from the land of eternal day,
Where the summer shall never die.
For high is the flight of the eagle.

" Little sparrow's world is his narrow lane,
He knoweth no sunshiny shore ;
His nestlings he feedeth and gathers his grain,
And yearneth for nothing more.
But high is the flight of the eagle.

" Now spring was breathing its healing breath,
With life teemed the earth and the sky ;
And fled were darkness and cold and death,
In the days now long gone by.
For high is the flight of the eagle.

" And the swallows came from the lands of light ;
In the belfry they built their nest, —
Their fledglings had there so wide a sight,
And there could so safely rest.
But high is the flight of the eagle.

" For they saw the sun in its glory rise,
. Saw the huge clouds chased by the gale ;

And they longed to bathe in those radiant skies,
As for the breeze longs the slackened sail.
For high is the flight of the eagle.

" One morn then, as loud chimed the sabbath-bell,
All the world seemed to beckon and sing ;
Then rose to the clouds one nestling, but fell
To the earth with a bruiséd wing.
For high is the flight of the eagle.

" Swift summer speeds, and the swallows flee
To the realms of summer and light.
Alas for him whose wing is not free
To follow them on their flight !
For high is the flight of the eagle.

" Yea, tenfold pity on him in whose breast
Live longings for light and spring,
But still must tarry in sparrow-nest,
Tarry with bruiséd wing.
For high is the flight of the eagle."

There was something almost ethereal in Rhyme-
Ola's voice; in the beginning of the song it was
clear and firm, but as he approached the end it
grew more and more tremulous, and at last the
tears broke through; he buried his face in his
hands and wept. Gunnar's sympathy was heart-

5   G

felt and genuine; before he knew it, he felt the
tears starting too.   He hardly understood the
whole depth of pathos in Rhyme-Ola's song; but
for all that he felt it none the less.   It inspired
him, as it were, with a vague but irresistible
longing to do something great, he knew not
what; and as he sat there musing over the sad
words, "tarry with bruiséd wing," the outer world
again receded, he forgot Rhyme-Ola's presence,
and his fancy again began its strange and capri-
cious play.   The words of the song, which were
still ringing in his ears, began to assume shape
and color, and to pass in a confused panorama
before his eyes.   Unconsciously, his thoughts
returned to what he had seen and heard in the
air and in the silence, and it was to him as if he
had never awakened, as if he was still wrapped
in the visions of his summer dream.   He was
startled by Rhyme-Ola's dark eyes staring at
him.   With an effort he fixed the scene in his
mind; and, as again the lake, the rocks, and the
distant Yokul lay before him, glittering in the
noonday, the song appeared far, far away, like a

dim recollection from some half-forgotten fireside
tale. The fireside led his thought to his grandmother; and as one thought followed another,
he at last wondered if Rhyme-Ola had any grandmother.

"Have you any grandmother, Rhyme-Ola?"
said he.

"Grandmother? Never had any."

Gunnar could hardly credit such an assertion;
and wishing for more satisfactory information, he
continued to ask the songster about his father
and mother and other family relations; but he received only evasive answers, and it was evident that
the subject was not agreeable. Now and then he
made a remark about the cattle or the weather,
and finally succeeded in bringing up another
theme of conversation. So they talked on for an
hour or more. Then Rhyme-Ola started to go.

"It is St. John's Eve to-morrow night," said
he, as he arose; "you will of course be at St.
John's Hill."

"I did not know it was St. John's Eve, but I
think I shall come."

And Rhyme-Ola walked off.

"Many thanks for your song," cried Gunnar after him.

"Thanks to yourself."

"You will come again very soon, won't you?"

"Very soon."

Here Rhyme-Ola was out of sight.

Gunnar again sat down on the rock, reviewing all the wonderful events of the day.

VII.

ST. JOHN'S EVE.

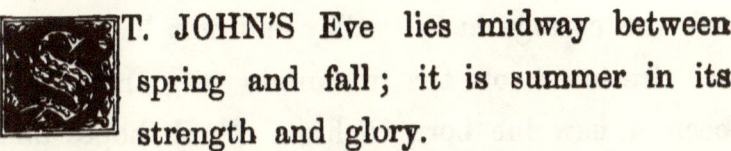T. JOHN'S Eve lies midway between spring and fall; it is summer in its strength and glory.

The day was far advanced, evening was drawing near. Gunnar· had again taken his station on the rock projecting into the lake, on the very same spot where Rhyme-Ola had found him the day before. On his knees rested a wooden board made of two rough fir-planks, whereon was spread out a large, square piece of thin, white birch-bark. In his hand he had a pencil, with which he drew on the bark. The cattle showed evident signs of impatience, for it was already milking-hour; but Gunnar was too much absorbed in his work even to be conscious of their presence. Many new, strange thoughts had been playing in his mind since Rhyme-Ola's visit. Still the sad and yet bold and rousing strain of the song kept ringing in his ear, now wakening him to life and action, now tuning his mind to blissful revery. When he had first left the cottage in the valley and first had drunk the freshness of the mountain air, there had been a new life born in him. Fresh hopes and longings had thronged his mind; Necken, the Hulder, and all that was fair to his childish fancy had suddenly become living realities, and he could often feel their enchanting presence, when the day fell warm and wondering over the highlands, and the air held its breath in anxious silence. Often had he spent hour after hour searching through the dark and half-hidden copse in the hope of catching a glimpse of some airy sprite. Never a loor-tone came floating over the plain, but he started to see if the Hulder might not be near; for he was sure the loor must be hers. True, shadows of doubt had been coming and passing, — shadows such as summer clouds throw on the forest when the sun is bright.

Like these they had again vanished, leaving the light the clearer for their presence. Then Rhyme-Ola came with his wondrous song. Although he did not sing of the Hulder, still either his song or himself in some strange manner again brought her to view. He had brought what had been lacking to make the chord full, the harmony complete; he had given form to the shapeless longings, had given rest to the restless chord. Gunnar no longer had need of looking without for the Hulder: into his own mind her image descended, clear and beautiful as the day. When he came to the saeter that night, he felt an irresistible desire to give expression to the powerful thoughts that moved within him. In the cottage at home he had always taken great delight in drawing the strange beings which lived in his fancy. For canvas he had used the cottage floor; paper he had never known. Since he had left home, he had often busied himself with projects for new drawings, but had never found an opportunity to execute his designs. To-night, however, he could allow nothing to defeat his purpose.

Having searched the saeter cottages from one
end to another, he finally discovered in the crevice of a beam a large pencil, which probably had
been left there by the carpenters.   Under one
of the beds lay a pile of birch-bark, which the
maids used for kindling-wood.   From this he se-
lected the largest and smoothest pieces, cut them
square, and found them even more suitable for his
purpose than anything he had hitherto tried.

It was late before Gunnar sought rest that
night; but the sun is late, too, at midsummer,
so there was nothing to remind him that midnight was drawing near. The next morning he
brought his half-finished drawing with him as
he started with the cattle, and took his seat on
his favorite rock, while the flocks were grazing
around on the lake-shore.   Now the day was
already leaning toward night; it had stolen away
like a dream, and he knew not how or where it
had gone.   Soon he should give the last touch
to his drawing; he saw that it was not finished,
but somehow or other he could not decide where
the finishing touch was needed.   It was the Hul-

der he had attempted to picture, fair as she stood
before his soul's eye. But the sketch before him
was but a fair mortal maiden : that unearthly
longing which gave its character to the tone of
her loor, and that unfathomable depth of her
eyes — that which really made her the Hulder —
he had failed to express. As he sat wondering
what the fault might be, a strong loor-tone shook
the air and came powerful upon him. He looked
up, and saw Brita, the fair-haired saeter-maid,
standing on a hillock a few hundred yards from
him, blowing her loor to call the cattle home.
Glancing at the sun, and seeing that it was far
past milking-hour, he quickly rose, put the loor
to his mouth, and gave such a blast that the
highlands echoed far and near. Brita's loor answered ; the cattle understood the welcome signal, and started for the saeter.

"Indeed, you are a nice cattle-boy!" cried
Brita, all flushed and out of breath, both from
her running and from indignation. "Did n't I
tell you to drive the flocks home early to-night?
and instead of that you keep them out more

than an hour after time. Now we shall have
to stay at home from the St. John's Hill, all of
us, only for your laziness, you hateful boy!"

Brita was justly indignant, and her words were
huddled forth with all the passionate flurry of
womanly wrath; but before she had finished she
found herself nearly crying at the prospect of
losing all the sport and merriment of the St.
John's Eve. Gunnar, conscious of his guilt, attempted no apology. As soon as they reached
the sacter, all the girls fell to milking as hard
as they could, and, much against his will, he
was obliged to assist them. When the cattle
were disposed of, they all started for the St.
John's Hill, which lay about midway between
the sacter and the valley. As they approached
the lake-shore, a pair of screaming loons flew
up from their nest among the rushes. It was
still bright day when they gained the pine region. A confused murmur rose from below; as
they came nearer they could distinguish the
strain of many violins, the song of women, and
the loud shouts of the men.

"No, indeed! I cannot run at this rate," groaned one of the girls, as she let herself drop down on a large, moss-grown stone. "If you have a mind to kill yourself for one dance, more or less, you may gladly do so. I shall not move one step farther until I am rested. Will you wait for me, Gunnar? for Brita hardly will, as long as she knows that Endre is dancing with some other girl, down on the hill."

Gunnar promised to wait.

"A poor set of girls we have here in the valley," said Brita, laughing, "who can hear the fiddles calling, and the lads shouting, and then can talk of rest. So tired I never was, and hope never to be." So saying, she ran down the steep road, and soon was out of sight. One of the girls followed, the other remained.

On the long and even slope from the highlands to the fjord, there is not seldom found an abrupt and steep projection, as if the mountain all of a sudden had thrust out its back, and determined to check the luxuriant vegetation below, which threatens to grow straight up over

its ears. From such a projection the eye has
a wide range, both upward to the mountains
and downward to the sea; for the pine is too
clumsy to climb, and the dwarf birch is neither
thick nor tall enough to hinder the sight. It
was on a ridge like this that Gunnar and the
saeter-maid were resting. From above they saw
the sun flooding with fire the western horizon,
and the purple-burning glaciers gleaming and
flashing. Below rose the waving crowns of the
pine forest, with its heavy green hue slightly
tinged with the flush of the sunset. Here and
there a tall, slender fir, forgetful of the winter
storms, lifted its airy head high above its hum-
bler fellows, and graciously nodded to some ad-
miring birches at its foot. In a wide opening
between the thick-growing pine-trunks lay the
St. John's Hill, which was, however, no hill, but
rather a large and sunlit glade. From the centre of this glade a huge bonfire, strangely wrest-
ling with the sunset, threw its glaring light upon
a dense mass of human life, whirling away over
the plain in wild enchantment. A thin, trans-

parent dusk seemed to rise from below, as the sun sunk deeper behind the glaciers. The forest drew its dark, steady outline on the horizon in effective contrast to the wild, flushing scene it embraced.

"Now I suppose you are rested," said Gunnar to the saeter-maid, who, like himself, seemed anxious to take an active part in the merriment below.

"Yes, thank you," said she, and they both arose.

After a short walk they arrived at the St. John's Hill, where he immediately lost sight of his companion; he hardly had time to realize where he was, before he felt himself hurried along into the midst of the crowd, where the stunning noise, the fire, and the strange people worked his senses up to such a pitch of excitement that at last he was not sure whether he was standing on his feet or his head. Another boy of about his own age, seeing how frightened he looked, went up to him, and fired his gun close to his ear. That suddenly brought him back to his senses; the blood rushed to his face, 'he clinched his fist, and dealt the boy a blow right under his left eye, so that he tumbled backwards. His opponent, however, jumped to his feet, and returned the blow with good effect. In the next moment they held each other in close embrace, and a hot fight ensued. The people flocked densely around them, encouraging them with shouts of approval; and they both fought as if their lives were at stake. At first, Gunnar seemed likely to be the loser, as he received more blows than he gave; but this rather added to his strength. The boy tried repeatedly to trip his foot, but he was on his guard; then he made a last rush at him, and they both fell, the boy under and Gunnar upon him. He was just rising, proud in the consciousness of his victory, when he saw a tall, grave man elbowing his way through the throng. The man walked rapidly up to the combatants, gave each of them a box on the ear, seized Gunnar's adversary by the arm, and carried him off. The people roared with laughter. Then, instead of pride in his victory, a feeling of shame stole over him. He ran away as fast as his feet could carry him, — away from the fire, the din, and the people. Tired and confused, he sank down on the soft moss, buried his face in his hands, and felt unhappy as he had never felt before.

He did not know how long he had been lying in this position, when he heard a well-known voice hard by. It was the voice of Ragnhild, the widow of Rimul's daughter. "Who was the boy who struck Lars?" said she.

"It was Gunnar, your cattle-boy," answered another voice, which he concluded to be that of Gudrun, the timid little girl he had seen at Rimul.

"Gunnar, our cattle-boy!"

. "Why, yes, of course. Lars came and fired his gun right in his ear, so it was no wonder he struck. I only wish he could be at hand when Lars strikes me; I never dare tell it to father, for when father strikes, he always strikes too hard, and then both mother and I cry."

Ragnhild was about to make some remark,

when Gunnar, who lay half concealed in the tall heather, raised himself on his elbows, to make them aware of his presence. Gudrun was a little frightened at his unexpected appearance, but Ragnhild walked up to him, sat down in the heather, and tried to open a conversation.

"Why do you like so much to fight?" said she.

Gunnar did not know what to answer; he felt as if he had something in his throat which nearly choked him. She fixed her large blue eyes upon him with an earnest, half-reproachful look. Then suddenly the tears rushed to his eyes, he pressed his burning face down in the moss, and wept as only a child can weep. He felt her hand on his head, and her fingers gliding through his hair. And there he lay weeping, until at last, consoled by Ragnhild's tenderness, he forgot the cause of his grief, and before long was engaged in a lively dispute with the little girls. Ragnhild, who had wondered ever since they first met at his strange story about Necken, now eagerly sought further information; and knowing little of the world of wonder, which he loved with life and soul, she could not conceal her doubt at the startling things he told her. He, of course, grew the more zealous, being opposed; and the girls, who were naturally no less superstitious than he, were only too willing to be persuaded. He was just deep in the wondrous tale of Saemund of Fagerlien and Margit of Elgerfold, when he was interrupted by the same tall man who had interfered in his combat an hour ago. He came to take Ragnhild and Gudrun home. "It is near midnight, children," said he, in a deep voice, "and the way homeward is long." And as they went they cried their good-night to him from the distance. He followed slowly and returned to the glade, where the fire was still blazing high, and the dance wilder than ever. There he met Rhyme-Ola, who told him that the boy he had fought with was Lars Henjum, and that the tall man who struck them was Atle, Lars's father.

After a time the music ceased, and the merry dancers, both lads and maidens, thronged round

the fire, where they sat down in a close ring, and
talked, jested, and laughed, little heeding the
waning hours and the solemn silence of the forest.
It was a gay scene, indeed, and one which would
have filled an artist with rapture. How fair did
those fresh, healthy faces appear, blushing, perhaps, with a little deeper tinge as the glow of the
fire fell over their features ! Here sat one leaning
forward, with his hands knit around his knees,
watching the flames in pensive silence ; there,
next to him, a merry couple, too much occupied
with each other to take notice of what was going
on around them. The young man was Endre, the
same who had opened the dance at the Rimul
saeter on the evening of their arrival at the highlands ; and who should the girl be but the bright-
eyed Brita, with the deep dimples in her cheeks ?
Endre must have been very interesting ; for
whenever he spoke, Brita laughed, blushed, and
now and then turned half away, as if to avoid
his gaze, while he sat bending over towards her,
intently watching her face.

As the night advanced, and the soft night-fog

spread over the forest, their minds were impercep-
tibly attuned to the supernatural. Now was the
time for wonder-tales and legends; and there was
none who could tell like Rhyme-Ola : there were
few who denied that. So Rhyme-Ola was called
upon for a story ; and there was no need of asking him twice, for there was nothing he liked better than story-telling. It was Rhyme-Ola's arrival
which interrupted Brita's and Endre's conversation. He came from behind them, and politely
asked to be admitted into the ring, for he hardly
could tell his story otherwise.

" Jump over, Rhyme-Ola," proposed Endre ; but
before the singer could have time to follow the
advice, he seized him round the waist, lifted him
high above his head, and amid a roar of laughter
from the company, put him down within the ring
right before the fire. Rhyme-Ola, being well used
to sport of this kind, took it in good part, straightened his little figure, winked with his sad eyes,
drew his mouth up to his customary smile, and
began his story.

When 'it was ended the narrator let his eyes

slowly glide from face to face along the listening circle, and saw, not without satisfaction, the frightened expressions and half-open mouths which sufficiently assured him that he had succeeded in securing attention. But in all that crowd there was hardly one who listened with so intense an interest as Gunnar. As soon as the tale had commenced he had joined the group and quietly taken his seat behind Brita's back, where he was still sitting when Rhyme-Ola found him.

"Gunnar," said Rhyme-Ola, "I have something I want to tell you." And he gently urged the boy on until they were out of hearing. Then, leaning against a large, white-stemmed birch-tree, he fixed his strange eyes on Gunnar and began again.

"I have been at Rimul to-day," said he, "and I have seen the widow." Here he hesitated, smiled his melancholy smile, and winked.

"I asked the widow of Rimul," he went on, "if she had not some cattle for me to watch too. She said she had. So, now I shall always be with you, Gunnar." And all his face laughed as he cried out the last words. Gunnar stood for a moment staring at his strange companion.

"What did you say?" asked he.

"From this time I shall always be with you," repeated Rhyme-Ola, laughing. "Now it is time to go home," added he; "it is very late, or, rather, very early."

Soon they were on their way, and reached the saeter at sunrise.

VIII.

GROWTH.

BLESS my soul! what is it the boy has been doing?" cried Brita, as her eyes fell upon the drawing which Gunnar had left standing before his bed. It was the morning after St. John's Eve, and Brita had come to wake him. Gunnar, before whose dreamy vision the variegated scenes and impressions of the night still were hovering, started up half frightened, rubbed his eyes, and asked what was the matter.

"Why, boy, what have you been doing?" repeated Brita in a tone which made Gunnar believe that it was something terrible he was suspected of having done; "have you been trying to make a picture of little Ragnhild?"

"No, indeed, I have not," asserted Gunnar,

still with a vague impression that such an attempt would be an unp rdonable boldness.

"Then, what does this mean?" said Brita, holding the drawing up before him. A stream of sunlight glided in through the airhole in the wall and struck the picture ; but it went farther and struck Gunnar too. What he had not known before, he knew now. It was not the Hulder : it was Ragnhild. He felt the blood mount to his temples, dropped his eyes like a convicted culprit, and remained silent.

Days came and days went, the summer sped, and autumn drew near. The wide highland with its freshness and freedom had become as a home to Gunnar; he longed no more for the valley ; nay, sometimes he even felt a strange dread of being closed in again under the shadow of those stern, inexorable mountains, now that his sight had been widened by the distance, and his thought had gained height and strength in the play with the infinite.

Rhyme-Ola was a great help to Gunnar, for a strong friendship bound them to each other.

The boy soon became familiar with his friend's peculiar ways, so they no longer disturbed him; and the songster, to whom sympathy and affection were new experiences, felt spring spread in his soul, and with every day that passed the boy became dearer to him. He sung him sad, and he sung him gay ; for there was power and depth in Rhyme-Ola's song : moreover, there was this peculiarity about it, that as soon as he struck the first note, the sky, the lake, and the whole landscape around seemed to fall in with it, and to assume the tone and color of the song. It was as much a part of the highland nature as the shrill cry of the loon or the hollow thunder of the avalanche · in the distant ravines. Thus Gunnar grew ; and Rhyme-Ola's song grew with him and into him, opening his ear to the unheard, his eye to the unseen, and lifting his fancy to bolder flight.

As long as the sun sent life and summer to the earth, Gunnar and his friend remained at the sæter watching the cattle. The cows were intrusted to Gunnar's care, while the singer gave his whole attention to the sheep and the goats. In the morning they would always start in different directions, the one following the eastern shore of the lake, and the other the western. At noon they would meet at the northern end, on the rock which had been the scene of their first encounter. Then, while the sun stood high and the cattle lay in their noon rest, Rhyme-Ola sat down and sung, and Gunnar would take his board and draw. He could never draw so well as when he heard those weird tunes ringing in his ears; then the mind teemed with great ideas, and the hand moved as of itself. At first it was mostly Hulders he drew, but at the end of another month he gave up these attempts as vain. Then his companion also changed his song; and now old heroic ballads gave a new turn to his mind and new subjects for his pencil. His illustrations of his old favorite story of the poor boy who married the princess gained him great praise wherever they were shown. Rhyme-Ola declared them absolutely un-rivalled. Thus encouraged, he for some time devoted himself to similar subjects, and peopled

6

his birch-bark with the loving virgins and gigantic heroes of the ballads.

The summer fled, like a delightful dream, from which you wake just in the moment when it is dearest to you, and you vainly grasp after it in its flight.

Before long Gunnar sat again in his old place on the floor at the fireside, in the long dark winter nights, giving life and shape to old Gunhild's never-ending stories and his own recollections from the summer. Rhyme-Ola was again roaming about from one end of the valley to another, as had always been his custom; he never had any scruples in accepting people's hospitality, as he always gave full return for what he received, and he well knew that his songs and tales made him everywhere welcome. The next summer they again watched the Rimul cattle together; and while the one sung the other drew, and they were happy in each other; for Gunnar's sympathy warmed his friend's lonely heart, and Rhyme-Ola's song continued to Gunnar an ever-flowing source of inspiration.

Now and then the widow of Rimul would come up to the saeter to see how the maids and the cattle were doing; and Ragnhild, her daughter, who had a great liking for the highlands and the saeter-life, always followed her on such occasions. It was the common opinion in the valley that Ingeborg Rimul still carried her head rather high, and there were those who prophesied that the time would surely come when she would learn to stoop. For the stiffest neck is the surest to be bent, said they; and if it does not bend, it will break.

Ragnhild seemed to have more of her father's disposition, had a smile and a kind word for everybody. She was never allowed to go out among other people, and she seldom saw children of her own age. Her cousin Gudrun Henjum was her only companion; for she was of the family. Gudrun had not seen twelve winters before Ingeborg Rimul asked her brother, Atle Henjum, if she might not just as well make Rimul her home altogether. Atle thought she might; for Gudrun and Ragnhild were very fond of each other. Thus it happened that, wherever the one came, there came the other also; and when they rode to the saeter, they would sit in two baskets, one on each side of the horse.

Brita had of course told the widow about Gunnar's picture, and once, when Ingeborg was at the saeter, she asked him to show it to her. She was much pleased with the likeness, praised the artist, and offered to buy the drawing; but Gunnar refused to sell it. A few weeks afterwards, however, when Ragnhild expressed her admiration for his art, he gave it to her. Then Ragnhild wished to see his other productions; he brought them and explained them to her and Gudrun, and they both took great delight in listening to him; for he told them, in his own simple and glowing language, of all the strange thoughts, hopes, and dreams which had prompted the ideas to these pictures. Also Rhyme-Ola's tales of Trolds and fairies did he draw to them in words and lines equally descriptive; and for many weeks to come the girls talked of nothing, when they were alone, but Gunnar and his wonderful stories. Before

long they also found themselves looking forward
with eagerness to their saeter visits; and Gunnar,
who took no less delight in telling than they did
in listening, could not help counting the days
from one meeting to another.

" I do wish Lars could tell such fine stories as
Gunnar does," exclaimed Gudrun one evening as
they were returning from the saeter.

" So do I," said Ragnhild, " but I rather wish
Gunnar could come to Rimul as often as Lars.
Lars can never talk about anything but horses
and fighting."

Now it was told for certain in the parish, that
Atle Henjum and Ingeborg Rimul had made an
agreement to have their children joined in marriage, when the time came, and they were old
enough to think of such things. For Henjum
and Rimul were only separated by the river, and
if, as the parents had agreed, both estates were
united under Lars Henjum, Atle's oldest son, he
would be the mightiest man in all that province,
and the power and influence of the family would
be secured for many coming generations. Who

had made Lars acquainted with this arrangement
it is difficult to tell; for his father had never been
heard to speak of it, except, perhaps, to his sister; but small pots may have long ears, as the
saying is, and when all the parish knew of it, it
would have been remarkable if it had not reached
Lars's ears too. Few people liked Lars, for he
took early to bragging, and he often showed that
he knew. too well whose son he was.

The next winter Gunnar was again hard at
work on his pictures, and although Henjumhei
was far away from the church-road, it soon was
rumored that Thor Henjumhei's son had taken to
the occupation of gentlefolks, and wanted to become a painter. And the good people shook their
heads; "for such things," said they, "are neither
right nor proper for a houseman's son to do, as
long as he is neither sick nor misshapen, and his
father has to work for him as steadily as a plough-
horse. But there is unrest in the blood," added
they; "Thor made a poor start himself, and Gunnar, his father, paid dearly enough for his folly."
On Sundays, after service, the parishioners always

congregate in the churchyard to greet kinsmen and friends, and discuss parish news; and it was certain enough that Gunnar Henjumhei's name fared 'ill on such occasions. At last the parish talk reached Gunhild's ear, and she made up her mind to consult her son about the matter; for she soon found out that Gunnar himself was very little concerned about it.

"It is well enough," said Gunhild, "to turn up your nose and say you don't care. But to people like us, who have to live by the work others please to give us, it is simply a question of living or starving."

But Gunnar never listened in that ear.

One night the boy had gone over to Rimul with some of his latest sketches and compositions, and had probably been invited to stay to supper. In the cottage Thor and his mother were sitting alone at their meal.

"I wonder where the boy is to-night," remarked Gunhild.

"Most likely at Rimul, with those pictures of his," said Thor.

A long pause.

"A handsome lad he is," commenced the grand-mother.

"Handsome enough; well-built frame; doubt if there is much inside of it."

"Bless you, son! don't you talk so unreasonably. A wonderful child he is and ever was, and a fine man he will make too. I could only wish that he sometimes would bear in mind that he is a houseman's son, and heed a little what people think and say about him."

A bitter smile passed over Thor's face, but he made no answer.

"Then I thought, Thor," continued his mother, "that Gunnar is old enough to be of some use to you now."

"So he is."

"The saying is, that his name fares ill on the tongues of the church-folk, because he sees his father working so hard, without offering to help him, and sticks so close to that picturing. That will never lead to anything, and moreover hardly becomes a houseman's son."

"Maybe you are right, mother."

"So I am, son; and it would be according to my wish if you asked the boy to-morrow to go out with you timber-felling, as would be right and proper for one of his birth."

The next morning Gunnar was asked to follow his father to the woods. He went, although much against his wish, as he was just at that time designing a grand historical composition which he was very anxious to take hold of. Henceforward he went lumbering in the winter, and herding the Rimul cattle in the summer, until he was old enough to prepare for confirmation;* for every boy and girl in the valley had to be confirmed, and the last six months before confirmation, they had to go to the parsonage to be instructed by the kind old pastor. Lars Henjum also prepared for confirmation that same winter, and so it happened that he and Gunnar often met at the parsonage.

* Every person in Norway is by law required to be baptized and confirmed in the Lutheran Church. Before confirmation the candidate has to undergo a public examination in Bible history and the doctrines of the Church.

It was a large, airy hall in which the "confirmation youth" met.   The window-panes were
very small and numerous, and had leaden sash-
es ; the walls were of roughly-hewn lumber ; and
in a corner stood a huge mangle, or rolling-press,
for smoothing linen.   On one side of the hall sat
all the boys on benches, one behind another ; on
the opposite side the young girls ; and the pastor
at a little table in the middle of the floor.   Right
before him lay a large, open Bible with massive
silver clasps, a yellow silk handkerchief, and a pair
of horn spectacles, which he frequently rubbed,
and sometimes put on his nose.   The pastor had
thin gray hair, and a large, smooth, benevolent
face, always with a pleasant smile on it.   He had
the faculty of making sermons out of everything ;
his texts he chose from everywhere, and often far
away from Luther's Catechism and Pontoppidan's
Explanations.   His object was, not to teach theory
and doctrine, but, as he said himself, to bring re-
ligion down to the axe and the plough ; and in
this he certainly was eminently successful.   In his
youth he had visited foreign countries, and evi-

dently once had cherished hopes of a grander lot than a country parsonage. Not that disappointment had imbittered him ; on the contrary, these glowing dreams of his youth had imparted a warmer flush to many dreary years to come ; and even now, when he was old and gray, this warm, youthful nature would often break through the official crust and shed a certain strong, poetic glow over all his thoughts and actions. It was from this man that Gunnar's artistic nature received its strongest and most decisive impulse. He had not been many times at the parsonage before the pastor's attention was attracted to him; for he made good answers, and his questions betokened a thoughtful and original mind. Then some one of the girls had told one of the pastor's daughters that the " Henjumhei boy," as he was commonly called, was such a wonder for making pictures ; and when, on request, he brought with him some of his sketches, the pastor praised them and asked his permission to take them in and show them to his family. The result of this was an invitation to dinner at the parsonage, which Gunnar, of course, was only too happy to accept. The pastor and the young ladies treated him with the greatest kindness, and gave him every possible encouragement to go on in the study of his art. In the evening they showed him a great many curious books, which he had never seen before, and beautiful engravings of foreign cities and countries, where there were flowers and sunshine all the year round. Gunnar was dumb with astonishment at all the wonderful things he heard and saw, and did not even remember that it was time to go home, until the old clock surprised him by striking midnight. When he bade them all good night, they gave him several books to take home, and paper to draw on.

This first visit to the parsonage was a great event in Gunnar's life ; for, from that time, his longing took a fresh start, and it grew and grew, until it outgrew every thought and emotion of his soul. He was seventeen years now, tall and slender, and fair to look at. His features were not strongly marked, but of a delicate and almost maidenly cut ; the expression was clear and open. His eyes were of the deepest blue, and had a kind of inward gaze, which,` especially when he smiled, impressed you as a happy consciousness of some beautiful vision within. Had he known the privilege, claimed by artists, of wearing the hair long, he might have been accused of affectation ; but as artists and their fashions were equally foreign to him, the peculiar cut of his hair, in violation of all parish laws, might be owing to an overruling sense of harmony in lines and proportions ; for the light, wavy contour of the hair certainly formed a favorable frame for his fair and youthful features.

Spring was again near, and the day came for his confirmation. It was a clear, blessed spring Sunday, — a day on which you might feel that it is sabbath, even if you did not know it. And to the young people, who were standing that morning at the little country church waiting for their pastor, it was sabbath in a peculiar sense. First came the deacon, and read the paper giving

the order* in which they were to stand in the
aisle during the catechising. Gunnar's name was
called first, Lars Henjum's second. Gunnar had
long been an object of envy among the other
boys, on account of the attention paid to him by
" gentlefolks"; but that the pastor should have
ventured such a breach on the traditions of the
parish as to put a houseman's son highest in the
aisle on a confirmation Sunday, was more than
any one had expected. And, of course, no one was
more zealous in denouncing Gunnar than Lars
Henjum; for, as he said, he was the man who
had been cheated. Thus it was with unholy feel-
ings that Lars approached the altar.

By and by the congregation assembled ; all the
men took their seats on the right side, the women
on the left. The youth were ranged in two long
rows, from the altar down to the door, the boys
standing beside the men's pews, and the girls op-

---

* It is regarded as a great honor to stand highest in the
aisle on confirmation Sunday. It is customary to have the
candidates arranged according to scholarship, but more than
proper regard is generally paid to the social position of the
parents.

posite. All were dressed in the national costume of the valley : the boys in short wool-colored jackets, scarlet silver-buttoned vests, and light tight-fitting breeches fastened at the knees with shining silver buckles ; while the girls, with their rich blond hair, their bright scarlet bodices, their snow-white linen sleeves and bosoms clasped with large silver brooches, their short black skirts with edges interwoven with green and red stripes, formed with their transitions and combinations of color the most charming picture that ever delighted a *genre*-painter's eye. In their hands they held their hymn-books and carefully folded white handkerchiefs.

Every child looks forward with many hopes and plans to the day of confirmation, for it is the distinct stepping-stone from childhood to youth ; beyond lie the dreams of womanhood and the rights of manhood. In this chiefly rests the solemnity of the rite.

When the hymns were sung and the catechising at an end, the venerable pastor addressed his simple, earnest words to the young,

exhorting them to remain ever faithful to their
baptismal vow, which they were this day to repeat
in the presence of the congregation. His words
came from the heart, and to the heart they
went. The girls wept, and many a boy struggled hard to keep back the unwelcome tears.
After the sermon they all knelt at the altar,
and while the pastor laid his hands upon their
heads, they made their vow to forsake the flesh,
the world, and the Devil. Then, when all were
gone, the pastor called Gunnar into his study,
where he talked long and earnestly with him
about his future. There was, said he, an academy of art in the capital; and if it was the wish
of both Gunnar and his father that he should
cultivate his talent in this direction, he would
be glad to do anything in his power to promote
his interests. From his university days he knew
many wealthy and influential people in the capital who would probably be willing to render
him assistance. Gunnar thanked the pastor for
his good advice, said he would consider his proposition, and before many weeks bring him back

an answer. But weeks came and went, and the
more he thought, the more he wavered; for
there was something that kept him back.

.The next year, Ragnhild and Gudrun were
confirmed.

IX.

THE SKEE-RACE.*

HE winter is pathless in the distant valleys of Norway, and it would be hard to live there if it were not for the skees. Therefore ministers, judges, and other officers of the government do all in their power to encourage the use of skees, and often hold

* Skees, or skier, are a peculiar kind of snow-shoes, generally from six to ten feet long, but only a few inches broad. They are made of tough pine-wood, and are smoothly polished on the under side to make them glide the more easily over the surface of the snow. In the middle there are bands to put the feet in, and the front end is strongly bent upward. This enables the skee, when in motion, to slide over hillocks, logs, and other obstacles, instead of thrusting against them. The skee only goes in straight lines; still, the runner can, even when moving with the utmost speed, change his course, at pleasure, by means of a long staff, which he carries for this purpose. Skees are especially convenient for sliding down hill, but are also for walking in deep snow far superior to the common American snow-shoes.

races, at which the best runner is rewarded with a fine bear-rifle or some other valuable prize. The judge of our valley was himself a good sportsman, and liked to see the young lads quick on their feet and firm on their legs. This winter (it was the second after Gunnar's confirmation) he had appointed a skee-race to take place on the steep hill near his house, and had invited all the young men in the parish to contend. The rifle he was to give himself, and it was of a new and very superior kind. In the evening there was to be a dance in the large court-hall, and the lad who took the prize was to have the right of choice among all the maidens, gardman's or houseman's daughter, and to open the dance.

The judge had a fine and large estate, the next east of Henjum; his fields gently sloped from the buildings down toward the fjord, but behind the mansion they took a sudden rise toward the mountains. The slope was steep and rough, and frequently broken by wood-piles and fences; and the track in which the skee-

runners were to test their skill was intention-
ally laid over the roughest part of the slope
and over every possible obstacle; for a fence
or a wood-pile made what is called "a good
jump."

It was about five o'clock in the afternoon.
The bright moonshine made the snow-covered
ground sparkle as if sprinkled with numberless
stars, and the restless aurora spread its glimmer-
ing blades of light like an immense heaven-
reaching fan. Now it circled the heavens from
the east to the western glaciers, now it folded
itself up into one single, luminous, quivering
blade, and now again it suddenly swept along
the horizon, so that you seemed to feel the
cold, fresh waft of the air in your face. The
peasants say that the aurora has to fan the
moon and the stars to make them blaze higher,
as at this season they must serve in place of
the sun. Here the extremes of nature meet;
never was light brighter than here, neither has
that place been found where darkness is blacker.
But this evening it was all light; the frost was

hard as flint and clear as crystal. From twenty
to thirty young lads, with their staves and skees
on their shoulders, were gathered at the foot of
the hill, and about double the number of young
girls were standing in little groups as spectators.

The umpires of the race were the judge and
his neighbor, Atle Henjum. The runners were
numbered, first the gardmen's sons, beginning
with Lars Henjum, then the housemen's sons.
The prize should belong to him who could go
over the track the greatest number of times
without falling; grace in running and indepen-
dence of the staff were also to be taken into
consideration. "All ready, boys!" cried the
judge; and the racers buttoned their jackets up
to the neck, pulled their fur-brimmed caps down
over their ears, and climbed up through the
deep snow to the crest of the hill. Having
reached it, they looked quite small from the
place where the spectators were standing; for
the hillside was nearly four hundred feet high,
and so steep that its white surface, when seen

from a distance, appeared very nearly like a per-
pendicular wall. The forest stood tall and grave
in the moonshine, with its dark outline on both
sides marking the skee-track; there were, at
proper intervals, four high "jumps," in which
it would take more than ordinarily strong legs
to keep their footing. When all preparations
were finished, the judge pulled out his watch
and note-book, tied his red silk handkerchief to
the end of his cane, and waved it thrice. Then
something dark was seen gliding down over the
glittering field of snow; the nearer it came, the
swifter it ran; now it touched the ground, now
again it seemed to shoot through the air, like an
arrow sent forth from a well-stretched bow-string.
In the twinkling of an eye it was past and
nearly out of sight down in the valley. "That
was Gunnar," whispered Ragnhild in Gudrun's
ear (for, of course, they were both there). "No
one can run the track like him." "No, it was
Lars," replied Gudrun; "he is number one on
the list."

"Hurrah! Well done!" cried the judge,

turning to Atle Henjum. " Heaven be praised, we have men in the valley yet! Truly, I half feared that the lad might not be found who could keep his footing in my neck-breaking track."

" The old Viking blood is not quite extinct yet," remarked Atle, with dignity; for it was Lars who had opened the contest. Now one after another tried; but some fell in the first, some in the second jump,* and single skees and broken staves shooting down the track told the spectators of the failures. Some, discouraged by the ill-luck of the most renowned runners in the parish, gave up without trying. At last there was but one left, and that was Gunnar Henjumhei. All stood waiting for him with breathless interest, for upon him depended the

* A fence, wood-pile, or any other elevation of the ground is made into a jump by filling up the space on its upper side with snow, so the skee may slide over it. On the lower side a good deal of the snow is generally taken away. Thus the skee-runner, coming in full speed down the hill, shoots into the air ; and it takes a good deal of skill and practice under such circumstances to come down on the feet without allowing the skees to lose their balance.

issue of the race. Something like a drifting
cloud was seen far up between the snow-hooded
pine-trees. As it came nearer the shape of a
man could be distinguished in the drift.

"O Ragnhild, you squeeze me so dreadfully,"
cried Gudrun in a subdued voice; but Ragnhild
heard nothing. "Ragnhild, please, Ragnhild, I
can hardly breathe." A chill gust of wind swept
by, and blew the cold snow into their faces. Ragnhild drew a long breath. A mighty hurrah rang
from mountain to mountain. The judge shook
his head: he did not know who had deserved
the prize. Gunnar came marching up the hillside, all covered with snow, and looking like a
wandering snow-image; his skees he had flung
over his shoulders. All the young people flocked
round him with cheers and greetings. He was
very hot and flushed, and his eyes looked eagerly
around, as if seeking something; they met Ragnhild's triumphant smile, which sufficiently assured him that she was happy with him in his
victory. But there were other eyes also that
were watching Ragnhild; and, suddenly, struck

with Lars's dark, ill-boding glance, she blushed and quickly turned away.

"Would you object to another race, boys?" asked the judge, addressing the two combatants.

"No!" cried they both in the same breath. "Gunnar will have to run first," added Lars; "my skee-band is broken, so I shall have to go and cut a new one." Gunnar declared himself willing to run first, and again climbed the hill.

"It is fearfully hot here," whispered Ragnhild to her cousin; "come, let us walk up along the track."

"Hot, Ragnhild?" And Gudrun looked extremely puzzled.

"Yes, come." Near the last great jump Ragnhild stopped, and leaned against a mighty fir, whose long, drooping branches, with their sparkling, frost-silvered needles, formed a kind of cage around them. Gudrun sat down in the snow, and looked up along the track. "There he is!" whispered she, eagerly. The girls were just stepping forward from behind the tree, when Ragnhild discovered the shape of a man on the other side, and in the same moment saw a large pine-branch gliding across the track a few rods above the jumps. There was no time to think. "O Lars!" shrieked she, and with an almost supernatural power she hurled the branch over against the man. Again a snow-cloud blustered, and swept by. The man gazed aghast before him, and, as if struck by lightning, fell backwards to the ground, — for it was Lars. There he lay for a long while; but when the girls were out of sight, he lifted his head warily, cast a furtive glance over to the great fir, and, rising to his feet, sneaked down towards the crowd. Another hurrah struck his ear; he hesitated for a moment, then turned slowly round and walked back into the woods.

That night there was searching and asking for Lars far and wide; but Lars was not to be found; and when the judge grew tired of waiting, the prize was awarded to Gunnar.

When the umpires and the young lads and maidens had betaken themselves to the dancing-hall, and the ale-horns were already passing round, there were still two remaining in the forest. The one was sitting in the snow, with her fair young face buried in her hands; the moonshine fell full upon her golden stream of hair; it was Ragnhild, and Gudrun's tearful eyes looked lovingly and pityingly on her.

"O Ragnhild, Ragnhild!" sobbed Gudrun, no longer able to master her emotion, "why did you never tell me? And I, who never thought it possible! If you could only have trusted in me, Ragnhild; for I do love you so much." And Gudrun knelt in the snow, threw her arms round her neck, and wept with her. Thus they sat, weeping their sorrow away, while the moon looked down on them in wonder.

"O dear, how foolish I am!" sighed Gudrun, as she rose, and shook the snow from her skirts. "Come, Ragnhild, let us go: it is too cold for you to be sitting here." The other wiped the tears from her eyes, and they both set out for the court-hall, where the dance was soon to begin. "Do you think anybody will notice that I have

cried ?" asked Ragnhild, rubbing her cheeks and
eyes with her apron, anxious to efface the marks
of the treacherous tears.

"O no, dear!" said Gudrun, taking a hand-
ful of snow and applying it to her eyes, which,
however, did not produce the desired effect. Slowly they walked down the steep hill towards the
court-hall, whence they could already hear the
alluring strain of the violins. They had both too
much to think of, therefore the walk was a silent
one. Only now and then Gudrun would draw her
arm still more tightly round Ragnhild's waist, and
Ragnhild would answer with a warm, speaking
look.

"Ragnhild, halloo!" The girls stopped and
looked doubtingly at each other, as if each one
expected the other to answer; for they well knew
that the voice was Gunnar's.

"Gudrun, halloo!" came the shout again, and
stronger than before; it struck the border of the
forest, rebounded again, and came sailing down
toward them. "Shall I answer?" whispered
Gudrun.

"Yes — O no, don't." But the counter-order either came late or was not heard; Gudrun had already answered.

"Halloo!" cried she, and a wanton echo played with her voice, tossed it against the mountain-side, and caught it again. Another call; and in the light of the moon they saw Gunnar's tall figure coming up the hill on his skees. With a long staff he pushed himself forward. Soon he was at their side. "Well met, girls!" cried he, gayly, as he jumped off his skees and extended one hand to each of them. "I was half afraid that Lars had already dragged you home, since I could not find you anywhere."

Here, suddenly struck with the grave expression of their countenances, and perhaps also discovering the marks of recent tears, he paused, and looked wonderingly at them. Ragnhild had a feeling that she ought to speak, but somehow or other both voice and words failed her. Then she raised her eyes and met his wondering gaze. "Ragnhild," said he, warmly, walking right up to her, "what has happened?"

"I am very glad you slid so well to-day, Gunnar," said she, evading the question.

"Are you, truly?"

"Yes," softly. How happy that word made him! Another pause; for that assurance was sweet to rest on. "The track was steep," remarked she after a while.

"So it was."

"I wonder you did not fall."

"Fall! O Ragnhild, I could slide down the steepest mountain-side, if only you would stand by and look at me." Something drove the blood to her cheek; he saw it and his courage grew; there came new fervor and manly reliance into his own voice. "I don't know why, Ragnhild, but whenever your eyes rest on me, I feel myself so strong, — so strong."

They were near the court-yard; the noise of the fiddles and the merriment within rose above his voice. Three men on skees came out from the yard and approached them. "Hurrah, boys! here we have the prize-racer," cried one of them. "Ah, fair Ragnhild of Rimul! You are racing

for a high prize there, Gunnar Henjumhei."
"Doubt if you will win in that race, Gunnar
Houseman's son," shouted another. "The track
is steep from Henjumhei to Rimul," said the
third; "the river flows swift between."

The three men had passed. It was long before
any one spoke. "How cold it is!" said Gudrun,
and shivered; and they all snivered. A stealthy
frost had crept between them. It froze Gunnar's
courage, it froze Ragnhild's life-hope. A houseman's son! On this day of his victory, so young ·
and so strong, and still only a houseman's son!
They were at the door of the court-hall. He
looked for Ragnhild, but she was gone. She also
had left him. Well, he was nothing but a houseman's son, and she the richest heiress in the
valley. She herself knew that too, of course.
The river flows deep between Henjumhei and
Rimul. The music from within came over him,
wild and exciting; and suddenly seized by the
wildness of the tones, he threw his head back,
sprang forward, and bounded into the hall. The
crowd made way for him as he came; up he

leaped again, grazed with his heel a beam in the ceiling,* and came firmly down on his feet in the centre of the dancing throng. The people rushed aside and formed a close ring around him. The men gave vent to their feeling in loud shouts of approbation, and the girls looked on in breathless admiration.

"A leap worthy of a Norseman!" said one of the old men, when the noise had subsided.

"O yes," cried Gunnar, with a defiant laugh, "worthy of a Norseman, worthy of even a — houseman's son! Ha, ha, ha! strike up a tune, and that a right lusty one." The music struck up, he swung about on his heel, caught the girl who stood nearest him round the waist, and whirled away with her, while her hair flew round her. Suddenly he stopped and gazed right into her face, and who should it be but Ragnhild?

---

* Among the peasantry in Norway, it is considered a test of great strength and manliness to kick the beam in a ceiling and come down without falling. Boys commence very early practising, and often acquire great skill in this particular branch of gymnastics. He is regarded as a weakling who cannot kick his own height.

She begged and tried to release herself from his arm, but he lifted her from the floor, made another leap, and danced away, so that the floor shook under them.

"Gunnar, Gunnar," whispered she, "please, Gunnar, let me go." He heard nothing. "Gunnar," begged she again, now already half surrendering, "only. think, what would mother say if she were here?" But now she also began to feel the spell of the dance. The walls, the roof, and the people began to whirl round her in a strange, bewildering circle; in one moment the music seemed to be winging its way to her from an unfathomable depth in an inconceivable, measureless distance, and in the next it was roaring and booming in her ears with the rush and din of an infinite cataract of tone. Unconsciously her feet moved to its measure, her heart beat to it, and she forgot her scruples, her fear, and everything but him in the bliss of the dance. For those Hulder-like tones of the Hardanger violin never fail to strike a responsive chord in the heart of a Norse woman. Gunnar knew

7 *

how to tread the springing dance, and no one
would deny him the rank of the first dancer in
the valley. Those who had been on the floor
when he began had retired to give place to him.
Some climbed upon the tables and benches along
the walls, in order to see better. And that was
a dance worth seeing. So at least the old men
thought, for louder grew their shouts at every
daring leap; and so the girls thought too, for
there was hardly one of them who did not wish
herself in the happy Ragnhild's place.

After the music had ceased, it was some time
before Ragnhild fully recovered her senses; she
still clung fast to Gunnar's arm, the floor seemed
to be heaving and sinking under her, and the
space was filled with a vague, distant hum.
"Come, let us go out," said he; "the fresh night-
air will do you good." The night was clear as
the day, the moon and the stars glittered over
the wide fields of snow, and the aurora borealis
flashed in endless variations. A cold rush of
air struck against them, and with every breath
he inhaled new strength and courage. Still the

whirling bliss of the dance throbbed in his veins, and he felt as if lifted above himself. And Ragnhild it was who walked there at his side, — Ragnhild herself, fairer than thought or dream could paint her. It was Ragnhild's hand he held so close in his. And was it not she who had been the hope, the life, and the soul of these many' aimless years? When he spoke, how he spoke, he knew not, but speak he did.

"Ragnhild," said he, warmly, "you know — that — Ragnhild, you know I always liked you very much." She let her eyes fall, blushed, but made no answer. "Ragnhild, you know that I always — always — loved you. Do you not, Ragnhild?"

"Yes, Gunnar, I do know it."

"Then, Ragnhild, tell me only that you love me too. There is nothing, no, I am sure there can be nothing in all the world, which I could not do, if I only knew that you loved me. Then all those pictures which I feel within me would come out into light; for they all came from you. Ragnhild, say that you love me."

"Gunnar, you have been dear to me — ever
— ever — since I can remember," whispered she,
hardly audibly, and struggling with her tears.
There lay a world of light before him.

Not far from the court-hall, down toward the
fjord, stood two huge fir-trees. They both had
. tall, naked trunks, and thick, bushy heads, and
they looked so much alike that people called
them the twin furs.   It was the saying, also,
that lovers often met there.   Between the trees
was nailed a rough piece of plank to sit on,
Here they stopped and sat down.   He laid his
arm round her waist, and drew her close up to
him; she leaned her head on his breast.   Then
he turned his eyes upward to the dark crowns
of the trees, and seemed lost in a stream of
thought.   The moonlight only shimmered through,
for the foliage was very thick.   Neither spoke;
they felt no need of words.   Silence is the truest language of bliss.   And she also looked up
into the heavy, moon-fretted mass overhead,
wondering what his thoughts might be.

"What a queer shape that tree has!" exclaimed she; "it looks like a huge Trold with three heads."

Then a light flashed upon him, and in a moment his whole past life lay before him, from the days of the saddle "Fox," and his grandmother's stories, to this night. "O Ragnhild," said he, looking longingly into her dewy eyes, "at last I have found my beautiful princess!" And that thought made him suddenly so glad that before he knew it he kissed her. For a moment she looked startled, almost frightened; but as her eyes again rested in his her face brightened into a happy, trustful smile. Now their thoughts and their words wandered to the past and to the future.

It was a happy, happy hour.

Gudrun had hardly been a minute off the floor, from the time she came inside the door. Thus it was some time before she was aware of Ragnhild's absence. But when there came a pause in the dance, and the time had arrived for the *stev*, she searched all over the house for her cousin, but without success. Soon she dis-

covered that Gunnar also was gone; for everybody was asking for him. He was wanted to
open the stev, as he had a fine voice, and a
good head for rhyming. Then, seized with fearful apprehensions, she rushed out of the hall,
and down the road, toward the fjord. She would
probably have taken no notice of the twin firs,
if Ragnhild had not seen her and called her.

"Why, Ragnhild," cried Gudrun, breathless
with fear and running, "how you have frightened me! I could not imagine what had become of you. Everybody is asking for you.
They want Gunnar to open the stev."

They all hurried back to the hall. Gudrun
might well wish to ask questions, but she dared
not; for she felt the truth, but was afraid of
it. They could not help seeing, when they entered the hall, that many curious glances were
directed toward them. But this rather roused
in both a spirit of defiance. Therefore, when
Gunnar was requested to begin the stev, he
chose Ragnhild for his partner, and she accepted. True, he was a houseman's son, but

he was not afraid. There was a giggling and
a whispering all round, as hand in hand they
stepped out on the floor. Young and old, lads
and maidens, thronged eagerly about them.
Had she not been so happy, perhaps she would
not have been so fair. But as she stood there,
in the warm flush of the torch-light, with her
rich, blond hair waving down over her shoulders, and with that veiled brightness in her eyes,
her beauty sprang upon you like a sudden wonder, and her presence was inspiration. And
Gunnar saw her; she loved him : what cared
he for all the world beside? Proudly he raised
his head and sang : —

Gunnar.   There standeth a birch in the lightsome lea,
Ragnhild. In the lightsome lea ;
Gunnar.   So fair she stands in the sunlight free,
Ragnhild. In the sunlight free ;
Both.   So fair she stands in the sunlight free.

Ragnhild. High up on the mountain there standeth a pine,
Gunnar.   There standeth a pine ;
Ragnhild. So stanchly grown and so tall and fine, —
Gunnar.   So tall and fine ;
Both.   So stanchly grown and so tall and fine.

Gunnar.	A maiden I know as fair as the day,
Ragnhild.	As fair as the day ;
Gunnar.	She shines like the birch in the sunlight's play,
Ragnhild.	In the sunlight's play ;
Both.	She shines like the birch in the sunlight's play.

Ragnhild.	I know a lad in the spring's glad light,
Gunnar.	In the spring's glad light ;
Ragnhild.	Far-seen as the pine on the mountain-height,
Gunnar.	On the mountain-height ;
Both.	Far-seen as the pine on the mountain-height.

Gunnar.	So bright and blue are the starry skies,
Ragnhild.	The starry skies ;
Gunnar.	But brighter and bluer that maiden's eyes,
Ragnhild.	That maiden's eyes ;
Both.	But brighter and bluer that maiden's eyes.

Ragnhild.	And his have a depth like the fjord, I know,
Gunnar.	The fjord, I know ;
Ragnhild.	Wherein the heavens their beauty show,
Gunnar.	Their beauty show ;
Both.	Wherein the heavens their beauty show.

Gunnar.	The birds each morn seek the forest-glade,
Ragnhild.	The forest-glade ;
Gunnar.	So flock my thoughts to that lily maid,
Ragnhild.	That lily maid ;
Both.	So flock my thoughts to that lily maid.

Ragnhild. The moss it clingeth so fast to the stone,
Gunnar. So fast to the stone ;
Ragnhild. So clingeth my soul to him alone,
Gunnar. To him alone ;
Both. So clingeth my soul to him alone.

Gunnar. Each brook sings its song, but forever the same,
Ragnhild. Forever the same ;
Gunnar. Forever my heart beats that maiden's name,
Ragnhild. That maiden's name ;
Both. Forever my heart beats that maiden's name.

Ragnhild. The plover hath but an only tone,
Gunnar. An only tone ;
Ragnhild. My life hath its love, and its love alone,
Gunnar. Its love alone ;
Both. My life hath its love, and its love alone.

Gunnar. The rivers all to the fjord they go,
Ragnhild. To the fjord they go ;
Gunnar. So may our lives then together flow,
Ragnhild. Together flow ;
Both. O, may our lives then together flow !

Here Gunnar stopped, made a leap toward Ragnhild, caught her round the waist, and again danced off with her, while a storm of voices joined in the last refrain, and loud shouts of admiration

K

followed them. For this was a stev that was
good for something; long time it was since so fine
a stev had been heard on this side the mountains.
Soon the dance became general, and lasted till
after midnight. Then the sleigh-bells and the
stamping of hoofs from without reminded the
merry guests that night was waning. There stood
the well-known swan-shaped sleigh from Henjum,
and the man on the box was Atle himself. Ragnhild and Gudrun were hurried into it, the whip
cracked, and the sleigh shot down over the star-
illumined fields of snow.

The splendor of the night was almost dazzling as
Gunnar came out from the crowded hall and again
stood under the open sky. A host of struggling
thoughts and sensations thronged upon him. He
was happy, O, so happy! at least, he tried to persuade himself that he was, but, strange to say, he
did not fully succeed. Was it not toward this
day his yearnings had pointed, and about which
his hopes had been clustering from year to year,
ever since he had been old enough to know what
yearning was? Was it not this day which had

been beckoning him from afar, and had shed light
upon his way like a star, and had he not followed
its guidance as faithfully and as trustingly as
those wise men of old? "Folly and nonsense,"
muttered he, "the night breeds nightly thoughts!"
With an effort he again brought Ragnhild's image
before his mind, jumped upon his skees, and darted down over the glittering snow. It bore him
toward the fjord. A sharp, chill wind swept up
the hillside, and rushed against him. "Houseman's son," cried the wind. Onward he hastened.
"Houseman's son," howled the wind after him.
Soon he reached the fjord, hurried on up toward
the river-mouth, and, coming to the Henjum boat-
house, stopped, and walked out to the end of the
pier, which stretched from the headland some
twenty to thirty feet out into the water. The
fjord lay sombre and restless before him. There
was evidently a storm raging in the ocean, for the
tide was unusually high, and the sky was darken-
ing from the west eastward. The mountain-peaks
stood there, stern and lofty as ever, with their
heads wrapped in hoods of cloud. Gunnar sat

down at the outer edge of the pier, with his feet
hanging listlessly over the water, which, in slow
and monotonous plashing, beat against the tim-
bers. Far out in the distance he could hear the
breakers roar among the rocky reefs; first, the
long, booming roll, then the slowly waning moan,
and the great hush, in which the billows pause to
listen to themselves. It is the heavy, deep-drawn
breath of the ocean. It was cold, but Gunnar
hardly felt it.

He again stepped into his skees and followed
the narrow road, as it wound its way from the
fjord up along the river. Down near the mouth,
between Henjum and Rimul, the river was frozen,
and could be crossed on the ice. Up at Henjumhei it was too swift to freeze. It was near daylight
when he reached the cottage. How small and
poor it looked! Never had he seen it so before;
— very different from Rimul. And how dark
and narrow it was all around it! At Rimul they
had always sunshine. Truly, the track is steep
from Henjumhei to Rimul; the river runs deep
between.

X.

PARISH GOSSIP.

FTER the skee-race, all the valley was talking about Gunnar Henjumhei and Ragnhild Rimul. Some people, who believed themselves well informed, knew for certain that there must be something between them, for it was evident enough whom they both alluded to in their stev; and even if that meant nothing, no one could help noticing that they sought each other's company more than was proper for persons so wide apart in birth and external circumstances. Others, again, thought the idea too preposterous, and supposed that, at least on Ragnhild's part, the fondness amounted to nothing more than a common friendship, which, however, might be bad enough; for all agreed that it was an unpardonable boldness in a low-

born houseman's son to cast his eyes upon a
maiden who was worth at least her own weight in
gold. At last the parish talk reached Atle Henjum's ear, and through him the widow of Rimul.

It was a Sunday forenoon. On the hearth
in the large, well-lighted sitting-room at Rimul
burned a lively wood-fire. The floor was strewn
with new juniper, spreading a fresh smell of clean-
liness throughout the room. The snow was too
deep for women on the church-road that morning;
therefore Ingeborg Rimul had the old silver-
clasped family Bible, where births, marriages, and
deaths had been faithfully recorded for many
generations, lying open on the table before her.
Her eyes fell upon the gospel for the day; reading that, she thought she might at least have
some idea of what the text of the sermon would
be. She was following down the page with her
finger while reading. And still it was hardly the
gospel which was foremost in her mind to-day;
for, whenever unobserved, her eyes wandered from
the book to her daughter, who was sitting at the
window, fair and Sunday clad, with her head

resting upon her hand, while with an absent look she gazed at the starry figures of the ice on the frozen window. There was no one who did not think Ragnhild beautiful. She was one of those who unconsciously draw all hearts to them. People said she most resembled her father's family. It was from him she had that gentleness of bearing and those blessed blue eyes, whose purity and depth bore in them a suggestion of the infinite; but the clear forehead, the strong chin, and that truly Northern luxuriance of blond hair were inheritances from the mother. A sad, almost painful expression passed over Ingeborg's face, as she sat silently watching her, — an expression which had long been strange to her features; but it was only momentary, and was soon exchanged for her wonted mien of undisturbed calmness and decision.

Heavy steps were heard in the outer hall, and the noise of some one stamping the snow from his feet. Both the women raised their eyes as the door opened and Atle Henjum stepped in. He went up to Ingeborg and shook hands; then he came to Ragnhild.

" Thanks for last meeting," said he.

" Thanks yourself," said they.

He took a seat on a bench next to his sister. " Bad weather for lumbering," remarked he. " I have two hundred dozen logs ready for floating, but shall probably have to wait until spring before getting them down, if it keeps on snowing at this rate."

" We are hardly better off than you, brother," answered the widow. " I am afraid we shall have to burn our fences for wood, if next week does not bring a change in the weather."

" Little need is there of such a waste, Ingeborg, as long as there is only the river between Henjum and Rimul."

" Many thanks for your offer, but it never was my way to borrow. I don't like to feel that I need anybody, not even my own brother."

For some time they all sat in silence, with their eyes fixed on the floor, as if lost in contemplation of the knots in the planks of the floor or the accidental shapes of the juniper-needles. Then at last Atle spoke. " Well," began he slowly and with emphasis, "that day is probably not far off when there shall be no river to separate Henjum from Rimul." He looked toward Ragnhild as he said this; and although her face was turned away from him, she felt that his eyes rested on her. She quickly rose and left the room. "This was what I came to speak to you about, Ingeborg," continued Atle; "you know it has long been a settled thing between us that Henjum and Rimul should some day be one estate, and the way to bring this about you also know. Now Lars is a stout, well-grown lad, and Ragnhild is no longer a child either. So, if you are willing, I do not see any reason why we should not make the wedding, and the sooner the better. No one knows how many his days will be, and it surely would be a comfort to both of us to see them together before we take our leave."

"Atle," said the widow of Rimul, "you have my word, and I thought you knew your sister well enough to feel assured that her word is as good as gold. I can see no reason for hurrying the wedding. We are both folk in our best age,

8

and strong as rocks, so there is but little proba-
bility of our dying for many years to come; and
even if one of us should be called away, there
would still be one left to execute the other's
will."

Atle found this reasonable, but still he had
other motives for wishing a speedy marriage;
and since his sister compelled him to speak
what he would rather not have told her, he
would no longer keep from her the rumors which
were circulating in the valley, and had found
their way to his ear. He was of course aware
that they had no foundation whatever, for tact
and self-respect had always been innate virtues
in their family; but still the girl was young,
and a mother's advice might teach her to avoid
even the appearances which could give occasion
for such foolish gossip. He also told her that
Lars, since his sudden disappearance at the skee-
race, had hardly seemed the same person. Late
the next morning, when he returned, he had refused to give any account of himself, and ever
since he had had a strange, bewildered look

about him. If Atle had believed in trolds and elf-maids, he should surely have supposed that Lars must have seen something of the kind on his night walk in the forest. Ingeborg exhorted her brother to be at ease; she should have no difficulty in bringing the affair to the desired result, if he only would give her time; for the first year there could at least be no question of marriage. The stern, calm assurance in Ingeborg's words and manner removed Atle's fears; he had no doubt her plan was the better, — a concession which he never made to any one but her. With regard to Gunnar, they both agreed that he must have forgotten who he was, and that it was their duty to give him a reminder, before his conceit should run away with him.

It was nearly four weeks after the skee-race, and in all this time Gunnar and Ragnhild had hardly seen each other. The only place where they met was at church, and there they had to keep as far away from each other as possible; for they both knew that the valley was full of rumors which, if they came to Ingeborg Rimul,

would cause them infinite trouble, and possibly
crush their hopes forever. Thus weeks went,
and months, and neither of them was happy.
Wherever Gunnar went, people would stick their
heads together and whisper; the young girls
giggled when they saw him, and among the
men there would fall many a cutting word. He
soon understood, too, that it was not by mere
accident that he overheard them. This, however, instead of weakening his courage, gave it
new growth; but it was not the healthy growth
fostered by a manly trust in his own strength.
He was well aware that people did not speak
to him as they spoke about him. Since he had
grown up he had never been much liked, as he
had always been what they called odd, which
meant that he was not quite like all others;
and in small communities there can be no crime
greater than oddity. Ragnhild Rimul was the
best match within four parishes round, and when
any one so far below her in birth cast his eyes
upon her, he must naturally rouse the jealousy
at least of those who might have similar inten-

tions. But these were not the only ones who felt hostile to Gunnar. Few were readier to denounce him than those of his own class, who had no lofty aspirations to lead them away from the beaten track of their fathers.

Then it happened that one afternoon he sat dreaming over a plot for a new composition. It was to be the scene from King Olaf Trygveson's Saga, where the king wakes on his bridal night and sees the shining dagger in the hand of Gudrun, his bride.

> " ' What is that,' King Olaf said,
> ' Gleams so bright above thy head ?
> Wherefore standest thou so white
> In pale moonlight ?'

> " ' 'T is the bodkin that I wear,
> When at night I bind my hair;
> It woke me falling on the floor :
> 'T is nothing more.' " *

Olaf, the bold, youthful king, who had roamed eastward and westward on his Viking voyages,

* *Vide* Longfellow's Saga of King Olaf, in Tales of a Wayside Inn.

and had come home to preach the gospel with
his sword, had always been a favorite with Gunnar, and this was not the first incident of the
hero's life which had tempted his artistic fancy.
But, strange to say, to-day the noble sea-king
seemed but a commonplace, uncouth barbarian,
and Gudrun, Ironbeard's fair daughter, a stiff,
theatrical figure, in which there was neither
grace, nor life, nor heroism. However much he
turned and twisted her, she still retained a pro-
voking mien of awkward consciousness, as if she
were standing up for the special purpose of having her picture taken. In vain he tried to bring
unity and harmony into the composition. An
hour passed, and struggling through the chaotic
shadows dawned slowly but surely a clearer and
better day. It had been long coming, but now
it stood cloudless and clear in its own light;
and Gunnar passed from thought into resolution,
from resolution into action. Strange that he
had not seen it long ago ! He sprang up, seized
his cap, and rushed out. The day was dim and
foggy. He reached the river, unmoored a boat,

and slowly worked his way between the large
blocks of floating ice, till he touched the Rimul
shore. Upon the hillside, under the leafless forest, lay the mansion wrapped in fog. As he
came nearer he could see the windows glittering
through the fog, but, as it were, with an expression of warning, not the bright smile with
which they were accustomed to greet him in
those happy days when, as a boy, he brought
his sketches to little Ragnhild, and from her
childlike delight drank strength and courage for
coming days. These memories now again urged
themselves upon him, and even for a moment
made him waver in his determination; but, as
if fleeing from his doubts, he hurried onward,
and at length left them behind. Truly it was
time that he should begin to act like a man.
Ragnhild loved him, loved him as only Ragnhild
could love; but, hard as the thought might be,
it was not to be denied that she was ashamed
to own him before men. And could he wonder?
Had he ever done anything to prove to the
world that he was entitled to its respect? And

still what a power he felt within him! He was not the man who would have a woman stoop to own him, who would see her blush at her love for him. All this would he tell Ragnhild this day, tell her that she was no longer bound by any promise to him, that he was now going far away, where she should hear of him no more until he had lived to be something great. Then, perhaps, some time in the far future, when he should have compelled the world to know him and to honor him, he would return to her, if such should be her wish; and if not, he would be gone forever.

These were Gunnar's thoughts, and as he passed through the gate into the Rimul yard, he wondered again that he had not had the courage to know this and to say it before now. He had hoped to meet Ragnhild in the yard, that he might speak to her alone. This was about the time when she was wont to go to the cow-stables with her milk-pails. So he waited for some minutes at the gate, but not seeing her he concluded that she must already have

gone, and that he would probably find her in
the stable. But on his way thither he met one
whom, to say the least, he would rather not
have met; there, on the barn-bridge,* stood the
widow of Rimul, stiff and tall, on the very
same spot where he had seen her eight years
before, when, as a twelve years' old boy, he had
come with his father to take charge of her cattle.
If she had been a marble statue, and had been
standing there ever since, she could hardly have
changed less. The same unshaken firmness and
decision in the lines about her mouth; the same
erect, commanding stature, the smooth, clear forehead; even the folds of her white semicircular
head-gear and the black wadmaal skirt were ap-
parently unchanged: and although Gunnar had
grown from a child to a man in those years, he
again felt all his courage deserting him as he
stood face to face with the widow of Rimul.
Indeed, the similarity of this occasion to the
one alluded to, for the moment struck him so

---

* The barn-bridge is a bridge built from the yard to the
second floor of the barn buildings, whence the hay and wheat
are cast down and stored in the lower story.

forcibly that he found it beyond his power to conquer that same boyish bashfulness and embarrassment which he had experienced at their first meeting. He had always prided himself that there was not the man in the parish of whom he was afraid; and yet here was a woman in whose presence he was and ever must remain a boy. This consciousness irritated him; with a vigorous effort he collected his scattered thoughts, and slowly and deliberately drew nearer. At the foot of the barn-bridge he stopped and took off his cap. "Thanks for last meeting," said he. The widow gave no heed to what he said, but continued giving her directions to the threshers who were at work in the barn.

"Do you call this threshing?" said she, severely, picking up a sheaf of rye from a large pile which the men had just been clearing off the floor. "Do you call this threshing, I say? Only look here" (and she shook the sheaf vigorously); "I would undertake to shake more than half a bushel of grain out of this pile which you pretend to have threshed. Mind you, men soon get their passports from Rimul, if they work that way."

Gunnar, supposing that he had been unobserved, took the last words as a warning to himself, and was already taking his departure when a sharp "Gunnar Henjumhei!" quickly called him back.

"It is damp weather to-day," stammered he, as he slowly drew nearer. A few steps from her he stopped, pulled off his cap again, and stood twirling it in his hands, expecting her to speak.

"Whom do you want to see?" asked she, having measured him with her eye from head to foot.

"Ragnhild, your daughter."

"Ragnhild, my daughter, has never yet been so pressed for wooers that she should have to take up with housemen's sons. So you will understand, Gunnar Henjumhei, that housemen's sons are no longer welcome at Rimul."

A quick pain, as if of a sudden sting, ran through his breast. The blood rushed to his face, and he had a proud answer ready; but as his glance fell upon the stern, stately woman whom he had always been taught to look up to as a kind of superior being, the words died upon his lips.

"She is Ragnhild's mother," thought he, and turned to go. He had just gained the foot of the barn-bridge when a loud, scornful laughter struck his ear. He stopped and looked back. There stood Lars Heujum in the barn-door, doubled up with laughter. This time it was hard to calm the boiling blood; and had it not been for the presence of Ragnhild's mother, Lars might have had occasion to regret that laughter before nightfall. So Gunnar started again; but no sooner had he turned his back on Lars than the laughter burst forth again, and grew louder and wilder with the distance, until at last it sounded like a defiant scream. This was more than he could bear. He had tried hard to master himself; now he knew not whither his feet bore him, until he stood face to face with Lars and Ingeborg of Rimul. He clinched his fist and thrust it close up to the offender's face. Lars forgot to laugh then, turned pale, and sought refuge behind the widow's back.

"Gunnar, Gunnar!" cried she; for even she was frightened when she met the wild fire in his eye. She was a woman; it would be a shame to strike when a woman begged for peace.

He sent Lars a fierce parting glance. "You and I will meet again," said he, and went.

The two remained standing on the same spot, half unconsciously following him with their eyes, until the last dim outline of his figure vanished in the fog.

"Lars," said Ingeborg, turning abruptly on her nephew, "you are a coward."

"I wonder if you would like to fight with a fellow like him, especially when he was in such a rage," replied Lars.

"You are a coward," repeated the widow, emphatically, as if she would bear no contradiction; and she turned again, and left him to his own reflections.

In April fog and April sleet the days creep slowly. Every day Gunnar looked longingly toward the mountains, wondering how that great world might be on the other side. Every morning awoke him with new resolutions and plans; every evening closed over a tale of withering courage and fading hopes; and only night brought him rest and consolation, when she let her dream-painted curtain fall over his slumber, like a *mirage* over the parched desert.

XI

THE WEDDING OF THE WILD-DUCK.

ERG was the name of a fine farm the next west of Rimul. Peer was the name of the man who owned the farm. But the church and the friendly little parsonage were on the Henjum side of the river, and in the summer, therefore, the fjord was the church-road of the Rimul people and all who lived on their side of the water. This Peer Berg was a very jovial man, and had a great many daughters, who, as he was wont to say himself, were the only crop he had ever succeeded in raising; in fact, there were more daughters on Berg than were needed to do the work about the place, and it was, therefore, not to be wondered at that Peer Berg never frowned on a wooer; the saying was, too, that both he and his wife had

quite a faculty for alluring that kind of folks
to the house.   Gunnar knew the Berg daughters;
for wherever there was dancing and merry-mak-
ing, they were as sure to be as the fiddlers.   As
far back as he could remember, the church-road
had never missed the "Wild-Ducks" from Berg,
as they were generally called, because they all
were dressed alike, were all fair and gay, and
where one went all the rest would invariably
follow.   Now one of the Wild-Ducks was to
be married to a rich old bachelor from the neighboring valley, and people knew that Peer Berg
intended to make a wedding the fame of which
should echo through seven parishes round.   Sum-
mons for the wedding were sent out far and wide,
and to Gunnar with the rest.

It was early in the morning when bride and
bridegroom from Berg with their nearest kinsfolk
cleared their boats, and set out for the church;
on the way one boat of wedding-guests after
another joined them, and by the time they
reached the landing-place in the "Parsonage
Bay" their party counted quite a goodly num-

ber. The air was fresh and singularly transparent, and the fjord, partaking of the all-pervading air-tone, glittered in changing tints of pale blue and a cool, delicate green. Now and then a faint tremor would skim along its mirror, like the quiver of a slight but delightful emotion. Toward the north, the mountains rose abruptly from the water, and with their snow-hooded heads loomed up into fantastic heights; irregular drifts of light, fog-like cloud hung or hovered about the lower crags. Westward the fjord described a wide curve, bounded by a lower plateau, which gradually ascended through the usual pine and birch regions into the eternal snow-fields of immeasurable dimensions; and through the clefts of the nearest peaks the view was opened into a mountain panorama of indescribable grandeur. There gigantic yokuls measured their strength with the heavens; wild glaciers shot their icy arms downwards, clutching the landscape in their cold embrace; and rapid, snow-fed rivers darted down between the precipices where only a misty spray, hovering over the chasm, traced their way toward the fjord.

About half-way between the church and the
mouth of the river a headland, overgrown with
birch and pine forest, ran far out into the fjord.
Here the first four boats of the bridal party
stopped on their homeward way to wait for
those which had been left behind; in one sat the
bride herself, with breastplate and silver crown
on her head, and at her side the bridegroom
shining in his best holiday trim, with rows of
silver buttons and buckles, according to the custom of the valley; in his hand he held an ancient
war-axe.   On the bench in front of them Peer
Berg and his merry wife had their places; and
next to them, again, two of the bridegroom's
nearest kin.   The second boat contained the remaining Wild-Ducks and other relatives and con-
nections; and the third and fourth, wedding-
guests and musicians.   But there were at least
nine or ten loads missing yet; for the wedding
at Berg was to be no ordinary one.   In the mean
time old Peer proposed to taste the wedding
brewage, and bade the musicians to strike up
so merry a tune that it should sing through

the bone and the marrow. "For fiddles, like hops, give strength to the beer," said he, "and then people from afar will hear that the bridal boats are coming." And swinging above his head a jug filled to the brim with strong home-brewed Hardanger-beer, he pledged the company, and quaffed the liquor to the last drop. "So did our old forefathers drink," cried he; "the horn might stand on either end if their lips had once touched it. And may it be said from this day, that the wedding-guests at Berg proved that they had the true old Norse blood in their veins." A turbulent applause followed this speech of Peer's, and amid music, singing, and laughter the beer-jugs passed from boat to boat and from hand to hand. Now and then a long, yoddling halloo came floating through the calm air, followed by a clear, manifold echo; and no sooner had the stillness closed over it than the merry voices from the boats again rose in louder and noisier chorus. All this time the bridal fleet was rapidly increasing, and for every fresh arrival the beer-jugs made another

complete round. No one drank without finding something or other to admire, whether it
were the liquor itself or the skilfully carved silver
jugs in which, as every one knew, Peer Berg took
no little pride ; indeed, they had been an heirloom in the family from immemorial times, and
the saying was that even kings had drunk from
them. There were now eighteen or nineteen
boats assembled about the point of the headland, and the twentieth and last was just drawing up its oars for a share of the beer and the
merriment. In the stern sat Gunnar, dreamily
gazing down into the deep, and at his side his
old friend Rhyme-Ola, his winking eyes fixed on
him with an anxious expression of almost moth-
erly care and tenderness. In his hands he held
some old, time-worn paper, to which he quickly
directed his attention whenever Gunnar made the
slightest motion, as if he were afraid of being
detected. When the customary greetings were
exchanged, the bridegroom asked Rhyme-Ola to
let the company hear his voice, and the singer,
as usual, readily complied. It was the old,

mournful tale of Young Kirsten and the Merman; and as he lent his rich, sympathetic voice to the simplicity of the ballad, its pathos became the more touching, and soon the tears glittered in many a tender-hearted maiden's eye.

There is a deep, unconscious romance in the daily life of the Norwegian peasant. One might look in vain for a scene like this throughout Europe, if for no other reason than because the *fjord* is a peculiarly Norwegian feature, being, in life, tone, and character, as different from the friths of Scotland and the bays of the Mediterranean as the hoary, rugged pines of the North are from those slender, smooth-grown things which in the South bear the same name. Imagine those graceful, strong-built boats, rocking over their own images reflected in the cool transparence of the fjord; the fresh, fair-haired maidens scattered in blooming clusters among the elderly, more sedately dressed matrons; and the old men, whose weather-worn faces and rugged, expressive features told of natures of the genuine mountain mould. The young lads sat on the row-benches, some with the still dripping oars poised under their knees, while they silently listened to the song; others bending eagerly forward or leaning on their elbows, dividing their attention between Rhyme-Ola and the tittering girls on the benches in front. They all wore red pointed caps, generally with the tassel hanging down over one side of the forehead, which gave a certain touch of roguishness and light-heartedness to their manly and clear-cut visages. And to complete the picture, there is Rhyme-Ola, as he sits aloft on the beer-kegs in the stern of the boat, now and then striking out with his ragged arms, and weeping and laughing according as the varying incidents of his song affect him. As a background to this scene stands the light birch forest glittering with its fresh sprouts, and filling the air with its springlike fragrance; behind this again the pines raise their dusky heads; and around the whole picture the mountains close their gigantic arms and warmly press forest, fjord, and bridal party to the mighty heart of Norway.

When the ballad was at an end, it was some time before any one spoke, for no one wished to be the first to break the silence.

"Always the same mournful tales," said at length one of the old men, but only half aloud, as if he were speaking to himself.

"Rhyme-Ola," cried one of the fiddlers, "why don't you learn to sing something jolly, instead of these sad old things, which could almost make a stone weep?"

"You might just as well tell the plover to sing like the lark," answered Rhyme-Ola.

"I love the old songs," said Ragnhild Rimul (for she was there also); "they always bring tears to my eyes, but sometimes I like better to cry than to laugh."

Peer Berg now signalled to the oarsmen, and the boats soon shot swiftly in through the fjord. In about an hour the whole company landed on the Berg pier, and marched in procession up to the wedding-house. First came the musicians, then the bride and bridegroom, and after them their parents and nearest kin. The guests formed the

rear. Among the last couples were Lars Henjum and Ragnhild ; last of all came Gunnar and
Rhyme-Ola.

Berg was an old-fashioned place, for Peer Berg
took a special pride in being old-fashioned. Coming up the hill from the water, Berg appeared
more like a small village than a single family
dwelling. The mansion itself in which Peer with
his wife and his Wild-Ducks resided, was of a
most peculiar shape. It was very large and
had two stories, the upper surrounded by a huge
balcony, which made it appear nearly twice as
broad as the lower. Over this balcony shot out
a most venerable slated roof, completely overgrown with moss, grass, and even shrubs of con-
siderable size ; the railing, which had once been
painted and skilfully carved, was so high and
so close that it afforded little or no room for
the daylight to peep in and cheer the dreary nest
of the Wild-Ducks. Round the mansion lay a
dozen smaller houses and cottages, scattered in
all directions; if they had grown out from the
soil of their own accord, they could hardly have

got into more awkward or more irregular posi-
tions. One looked north, another west, a third
southeast, and no two lay parallel or with their
gables facing each other. Every one of these
houses, however, had been erected for some special purpose. First, there were, of course, the
barns and the stables, which in size and respect-
ability nearly rivalled the mansion. Quite in-
dispensable were the servant-hall, the sheepfold,
and the wash-house ; and without forge and flax-
house Berg could hardly have kept up its repu-
tation as a model establishment.

With gay music and noisy laughter and merriment, the bridal procession passed into the
yard, where from the steps of the mansion they
were greeted by the master of ceremonies in a
high-flown speech of congratulation. The doors
were then thrown wide open, and soon like a
swelling tide the crowd rolled through the house,
and the lofty halls shook with the hum and
din of the festivity. For at such times the
Norsemen are in their lustiest mood ; then the
old Saga-spirit is kindled again within them ;

and let him beware who durst say then that the
Viking blood of the North is extinct. The festal
hall at Berg, which occupied the whole lower
floor of the building, was decorated for the occasion with fresh leaves and birch branches, for
the birch is the bride of the trees ; but as it'
was still early in the season, it was necessary to
keep up a fire on the open hearth. This hearth
might indeed, in more than one sense, be said to
have given a certain homely color to everything
present, not only in the remoter sense, as being
the gathering-place of the family in the long winter evenings, but also in a far nearer one ; its
smoke had, perhaps for more than a century,
been equally · shared by the chimney and the
room, and had settled in the form of shining
soot on walls, rafters, and ceiling. Two long
tables extended across the length of the hall
from one wall to another, laden with the most
tempting dishes. The seats of honor, of course,
belonged to bride and bridegroom, and they
having taken their places, the master of ceremonies urged the guests to the tables and ar-

ranged them in their proper order in accordance with their relative dignity or their rela-
tionship or acquaintance with the bride. Now
the blessing was pronounced and the meal began. It was evident enough that the boating
and the march had whetted the guests' appe-
tites; huge trays of cream-porridge, masses of
dried beef, and enormous wheaten loaves dis-
appeared with astonishing rapidity. Toast upon
toast was drunk, lively speeches made and heartily applauded, tales and legends told, and a
tone of hearty, good-humored merriment prevailed. The meal was a long one; when the feast-
ers rose from the tables it was already dusk.
In the course of the afternoon the weather had
changed; now it was blowing hard, and the
wind was driving huge masses of cloud in through
the mountain gorges. Shadows sank over the
valley, the torches were lit in the wedding-
house, and a lusty wood-fire crackled and roared
on the hearth. Then the tables were removed,
the music began, and bride and bridegroom
trod the springing dance together, according to

ancient custom ; others soon followed, and before long the floors and the walls creaked and the
flames of the torches rose and flickered in fit-
ful motion, as the whirling air-currents seized
and released them. Those of the men who
did not dance joined the crowd round the beer-
barrels, which stood in the corner opposite the
hearth, and there slaked their thirst with the
strong, home-brewed drink which Norsemen have
always loved so well, and fell into friendly chat
about the result of the late fishery or the proba-
bilities for a favorable lumber and grain year.

It was late, near midnight. The storm was
growing wilder without, the dance within. Clouds
of smoke and dust arose ; and as the hour of
midnight drew near, the music of the violins grew
wilder and more exciting.

All the evening Lars Henjum had been hovering near Ragnhild, as if watching her ; and
Gunnar, who rather wished to keep as far away
as possible from Lars, had not spoken to her
since her arrival. Now, by chance, she was
standing next to him in the crowd ; Lars had

betaken himself to the beer-vessel, which, it was clear enough, he had already visited too often. As Gunnar stood there he felt a strange sensation steal over him. Ragnhild seemed to be as far away from him as if he had only known her slightly, as if their whole past, with their love and happiness, had only been a strange, feverish dream, from which they had now both waked up to the clear reality. He glanced over to Ragnhild and met a long, unspeakably sad look resting on him. Then like an electric shock, a great, gushing warmth shot from his heart and diffused itself through every remotest vein and fibre. The fog-veil of doubt was gone; he was again in the power of his dream, and in the very excess of his emotion ; forgetting all but her, he seized her hand, bent over her, and whispered, " Ragnhild, dearest, do you know me ? " It was an absurd question, and he was aware of that himself in the very next minute, but then it was already too late. She, however, had but little difficulty in understanding it ; for she only seized his other hand too, turned on him a' face beaming with joyful radiance, and said softly, " Gunnar, where have you been so long?" Instead of an answer, he flung his arms around her waist, lifted her up from the floor with a powerful grasp, and away they went like a whirlwind.

"A devil of a fellow in the dance, that Gunnar Henjumhei," said one of the lads at the beer-vessel to Lars, who happened to be his next neighbor; "never saw I a brisker lad on a dancing-floor as far back as my memory goes. And it is plain enough that the girls think the same." Lars heard it, he saw Gunnar's daring leap, saw Raguhild bending trustfully towards him, and heard the loud shouts of admiration. In another moment he imagined that all eyes were directed towards himself, and his suspicion read a pitying sneer in all faces.

"No use for you to try there any longer," cried a young fellow, coming up to him, and in the loving mood of half-intoxication laying both his arms round his neck; "it is clear the houseman's boy has got the upper hand of you."

"And if you did try," interposed another, "all
you would gain would be a sound thrashing; and
you always were very careful about your skin,
Lars."

Lars bit his lip. Every word went through
him like a poisonous sting, but he made no
answer. The bridegroom had gone to give the
fiddlers a jug of beer, and the music had stopped.
Ragnhild sat hot and flushed on a bench by the
wall, and Gudrun stood bending over her and
eagerly whispering in her ear. Gunnar walked-
towards the door, and Lars followed a few steps
after, — the two lads at some distance. "Now
there will be sport, boys," said they, laughing.

Gunnar stood on the outer stairs, peering into
the dark, impenetrable night. The storm had
now reached its height; the wind howled from
overhead through the narrow mountain gorges;
it roared and shrieked from below, and died away
in long, despairing cries. Then it paused as if to
draw its breath, and there was a great, gigantic
calm, and again it burst forth with increased
violence. To him it was a relief to hear the

storm, it was a comfort to feel its power; for in his own breast there was a storm raging too. When, ah! when should he summon the courage to break all the ties that bound him to the past? Before him lay the wide future, great and promising. O, should he never reach that future? The storm made a fearful rush; the building trembled; something heavy fell over Gunnar's neck, and he tumbled headlong down into the yard. His first thought was that a plank torn loose by the wind had struck him; but by the light from the windows he saw a man leap down the steps after him; he sprang up and prepared to meet him, for he knew the man. "I might have known it was you, Lars Henjum," cried he, "for the blow was from behind."

When Lars saw his rival on his feet he paused for a moment, until a loud, scornful laugh from the spectators again kindled his ire.

"I knew you would be afraid, Lars Henjum," shouted a voice from the crowd.

Gunnar was just turning to receive Lars when a blow, heavier than the first, struck him from behind over his left ear. The darkness was thick, and Lars took advantage of the darkness.

The flaring, unsteady light of a few torches struggled with the gloom; men and women, young and old, pressed out with burning sticks and firebrands in their hands, and soon the wedding-guests had formed a close ring around the combatants, and stared with large eyes at the wild and bloody play; for they knew that the end of such a scene is always blood. At windows and doors crowds of young maidens watched the fighters, with fright and eager interest painted in their youthful faces, and clasped each other more tightly for every blow that fell.

By the light of the burning logs Gunnar now found his opponent. Wildly they rushed at each other, and wild was the combat that followed. Revenge, long-cherished hatred, burned in Lars's eye; and as the memory of past insults returned, the blood ran hotter through Gunnar's veins. The blows came quick and strong on either side, and it would have been hard to tell who gave and who received the most. At last a well-directed

blow struck Lars in the head; the blood streamed
from his mouth and nostrils, he reeled and fell
backward. A subdued murmur ran through the
crowd. Two men sprang forward, bent over him,
and asked if he was much hurt. Gunnar was
about to go, when suddenly he saw the wounded
man leap to his feet, a long knife gleaming in his
hand; in the twinkling of an eye he was again at
his side; he wrung the weapon from his grasp,
and held it threatening over his head. "Beg
now for your life, you cowardly wretch!" cried
he, pale with rage.

Lars foamed; he made a rush for the knife,
but, missing it, he flung his arms round Gunnar's
waist and struggled to throw him. Gunnar strove
to free himself. In the contest, Lars's foot slipped;
they both tumbled to the ground. A shooting
pain ran through Lars's body; in another moment he felt nothing. A red stream gushed from
his side; he had fallen on his own knife. Gunnar rose slowly, saw and shuddered. The last
gleam of the torches flickered, dying.

Wildly howled the storm, but over the storm

arose a helpless shriek of despair. "O Gunnar, Gunnar, what hast thou done?" And Ragnhild sprang from the stairs, frantically pressed onward through the throng, and flung herself upon Lars's bloody body. She lifted her eyes to Gunnar with horror. "O Gunnar, may God be merciful to thee!"

The last spark was quenched. Night lay before him, night behind him. He turned towards the night — and fled. -

XII.

THREE YEARS LATER.

THREE years are a long time to look forward to, but how short they appear when once they are past! That this was Ragnhild's experience, she half reluctantly confessed to herself, as in the third spring after the long-remembered Berg wedding she wandered with her flocks to the mountains, where the old saeter cottages stood ready to receive her. And still, how wretched had she been in the first months after he had left her, how slowly and miserably had the days crept along! She had said that she would nevermore be happy, and happy she had not been ; but time, the healer of all wounds, had also blunted the sting of her sorrow. She no longer thought of Gunnar with pain or regret ; for her faith in him was great, and as the echo of his many and, as she now thought, wonderful words rung in her memory, she was even at times filled with an heroic devotion which made her strong to bear many a hard struggle which was to come.

Lars seemed to have grown much gentler since the affray at the wedding. He had been obliged to keep his bed for months, and it had even for some time been doubtful whether he was to regain his health at all. Of marriage there had been little said of late; and if people had not known both Atle Henjum and his sister so well, they might have supposed that the whole plan had been abandoned long ago. But Atle had been waiting for a favorable moment. This he now believed to have come; Ragnhild was composed and cheerful, Lars again as strong as ever, and, to make everything complete, the fishery had yielded this year nearly twice as much as usual, so the widow would be fully able to make a magnificent wedding, and that without touching either bank-book or the silver dollars on the bottom of her chests. Lars had accordingly set

out again for a visit to Rimul; and had he come
an hour earlier, he would probably have found
Raguhild at home. Now he came in vain.

The little cottage at Henjumhei looked cheer-
less and desolate since Gunnar had gone. The
rock still stood frowning over it; the overhanging
birch-trees still shook their yellow flower-dust
upon its roof, and wafted their spring breath in
through the open windows; the brisk river had not
yet ceased to shower its cold spray over its walls;
and yet, if you happened to enter, you would
hardly have said that it was the same cottage you
had seen years ago. There sat old Gunhild on
the hearth, and spun early and late, spun and
spun day after day, and never tired. Never
tired? Perhaps, if you looked more closely, you
would find that three years had wrought great
changes in old Gunhild. She is no longer the
cheerful, vigorous woman she used to be. She
talks very little now, for she has no one to talk
with. Thor was always a man of few words, and
now they are fewer than ever. Moreover he
spends all his day in field and forest; and when

he comes home late at night, hungry and tired, it is only to sit down in the fireside corner and there smoke on in silence, until sleep comes and makes the silence deeper. They had heard from Gunnar only twice in the three years he had been gone. In the first letter, which came some six or seven months after his departure, he had told them of his nightly flight from the valley, of his long wanderings and many hardships before he reached the capital and was finally admitted to the Academy of Art. The second letter was filled with enthusiastic praises of his friend Herr Vogt, a young man who was studying at the University, and who, from the time of their first meeting, had never ceased to shower upon him new tokens of regard. Time and daily intercourse had now ripened their intimacy into the warmest and sincerest friendship. Vogt was the son of a wealthy clergyman, who lived at some distance from the city, and Gunnar had received repeated invitations to spend his vacation at his home, which, however, for some reason or other he had declined. He had hitherto made his way by giving lessons in drawing, and by selling his sketches and compositions to illustrated papers. About Ragnhild he wrote not a word.

Strange it may seem that, in spite of Gunnar's success and happiness, his grandmother mourned him almost as if he had been dead. "Was it not what I always said, Thor, that that picture business would be sure to lead the child astray? But you never would listen to me, you Thor, when I told you to set the boy to honest work. There is no blessing in stepping beyond one's own station, my father used to say; and sure enough, there can come no lasting blessing from it either, Thor."

"It is often hard to tell where one's station is," Thor would answer.

One day he had been helping the girls to get the saeter cottages in order; and as there were a hundred things to do, and he the surest hand to do them, time had slipped by unnoticed, and the sun had already risen before he was on his homeward way: for sunset and sunrise follow close in each other's track in the month of midsummer.

As he passed the parsonage, he saw the old pastor walking in his garden, with slippers and dressing-gown, and a long-stemmed meerschaum pipe in his mouth.

"Good morning, Thor," said the pastor, with a friendly nod.

"Good morning. The pastor is early on foot to-day." And Thor pulled his red pointed cap from his head and held it respectfully in his hand, while the pastor addressed him.

"When one gets old one cannot always sleep at pleasure; and when light and darkness are no longer the distinctions between day and night, one is often tempted to get up both in season and out of season, according as wakefulness or weariness bids. In sleepless nights, however, I always have something to go by. As soon as I hear my hens cackling in the yard, I know the hour, and then there is no longer any question about staying in bed."

"I think the pastor once told me," observed Thor, taking a few steps forward, and leaning over the railing, "that he was always a light

N

sleeper. And when a man has so much in his
head as we know the pastor has, it is no wonder
that he finds little time for rest."

"But how with yourself, Thor? Age seems to
be gaining on you fast. You do not look half as
vigorous as you did a few years ago."

"One has to take things as they come." Here
Thor paused, raised his head abruptly, and looked
full into the pastor's face. "I suppose every
one has his share of troubles," he added, rather
hurriedly.

"Come in, Thor," and the minister opened the
garden gate; "come and sit down with me on
this bench here. It is a very long time since we
had a good talk together."

Thor entered and took a seat at the farther
end of the bench.

"I do not wish to intrude on you," continued
the pastor, striking a match on the bench, and
proceeding to light his pipe, which during the
conversation had been neglected. "I have no
intention of being inquisitive; but as your pastor,
I might perhaps be able to bring you aid and

counsel in the sorrows and troubles which beset you." Although thus invited to speak, Thor for some time remained silent, while the minister, with eager sympathy, watched the struggling emotions in his rugged features. It was not Thor's habit to speak; sympathy and confidence were quite unknown things to him.

"Pastor," he broke forth at last, and his voice trembled as he spoke, "you may remember Gunnar, my son. God knows I miss him very much." A peasant's thought is simple, and simple is his way of uttering it; but the minister saw through Thor's rough speech into the deep, loving nature beyond.

"Thor," said he, "I do not wonder that you miss your son; I confess, I often miss him myself. But then we must believe that God knows what is best for us all. And as regards Gunnar, I can give you great proofs that God holds his protecting hand over him. It was not for nothing I called you as you passed. Only look here!" The pastor pulled a letter and a newspaper out of his breast-pocket, and handed both to the peasant, while kindness and triumphant joy beamed forth from his countenance. "But wait a minute," continued he, "perhaps I had better take the paper, and if you would like to listen, I will read you something that may possibly interest you."

"I am not very good at letters," answered Thor, quietly. "I should like much if the pastor would be kind enough to read."

The other unfolded the paper and began : "The gold medal of the Academy of Art was this year awarded Mr. Gunnar Thorson Henjumhei, from the parish of T—— in Bergen Stift ; and a stipend for two years of foreign travel, to which this prize entitles him, will be conferred on him from August 1st, prox. Never, since the earliest days of the Academy, has an opportunity been afforded us of expressing a heartier approval of its decisions than on this occasion. Mr. Henjumhei is evidently a genius of no ordinary scope, and we dare confidently predict for him a place among the stars of the first magnitude, on the northern horizon of art. This is certainly much to say, but not too much ; for even the slightest glance at his Hulder (now on exhibition in the Academy) will convince the beholder that here is one of the favored few whom Nature has truly admitted into her confidence. Judged, however, by the strictest rules of art, the Hulder is not perfect, and perhaps far from perfect. But it is not conventional perfection we ask from our young artists. Mr. Henjumhei's Hulder possesses qualities compared with which, we had nearly said, even perfection would be of small account. The Hulder, in spite of imperfect foreshortenings and unwieldy drapery, is all instinct with the native fire of genius, and glows with a life which neither rules nor teachings could impart. The weird grandeur of the tradition could never have found a happier and more poetic expression than in those unfathomable, inward-looking eyes, in the harmoniously dramatic gesture of the raised hand, suggesting the idea that she is listening to some word or sound which, we feel sure, none but herself can hear, —

'To the breathless, anxious secret
Which ever must rest untold.'

And again, the light, sportful airiness, the deep, nameless longings, which, as they are blended in our popular superstition, give such a rich charm to this legendary being, — these are traits which the artist can well feel and express, but are of too subtile a nature for the critic to dissect and analyze. She is, as the ballad expresses it, 'the grace of the sunshine to the fir-tree's grotesqueness wed.'

" Before closing our notice, we shall in confidence relate what a bird has sung to us, namely, that Mr. Henjumhei caught the inspiration for his Hulder from some fair damsel in his native valley, to whom the picture in some points is said to bear a striking resemblance. If true, we will hope, in the interest of art, that he may soon find the charm to bind the wayward sprite. For, in sooth, he is a youth of whom any damsel, yea, old Norway herself, may justly be proud."

The pastor's incorrigible pipe had again gone out during the reading. While lighting it, his eyes were firmly riveted on his listener. Thor sat immovable as a statue; but a tear trembled

in his eyelid, and stole down his weather-fur-
rowed cheek.

"Good by, pastor," said he, rose quickly, and
went.

It was about seven o'clock in the morning
when Thor saw his cottage peeping forth between the light birch-trees. The night must
have been very damp; every tiny leaf and sprig
was hung with glittering dew-drops, and as the
sun smote them they played and sparkled as
from a luminous life within them. Thor looked
up, took two steps backward, shaded his eyes
with his hand, and gazed again. For fifty years
had he lived in that cottage, and how many a
time in those years the sun and the dew had
lent it their beauty! To him it was as if to-day
he saw it for the first time, at least since those
early years he had struggled so bravely to forget.
On the bench before the door sat his old mother with her knitting-work. "Poor thing," muttered he, "she wants to do everything for the
best. But well for the boy that he was stronger
than his father, or rather that a stronger hand

came in between him and us. 'A youth whom
old Norway herself may justly be proud of,'"
added he, musingly. "I knew well there was
the right mettle in him."

Then, of course, Thor hastened to his mother
with his news, that she might also know and
share his joy. No, his joy was one which none
but himself could feel, and none but his God
should share it with him. So he wandered down
toward the river, seated himself on a large moss-
grown stone, where a heavy-browed fir stooped out
over the rapids, and watched the strong, tumult-
uous life of the whirling waters.

The sun already stood high in the heavens,
when old Gunhild, lifting her eyes from her
knitting, and adjusting her spectacles, which
had slid down to the tip of her nose, saw her
son coming up toward the bench where she sat.
Her quick eye caught the change in him. A
calm, trustful happiness pervaded his whole being, and beamed forth from his countenance.

"Son," said she, "I should say that you must
bring good news from the saeter."

"So I do, mother," replied he, "and from farther off too than the saeter."

"Thor," cried she, dropping her knitting in her lap, "has the boy come?"

"Not that I know," said Thor, "but here, let him speak for himself." And he took the letter out from his inside waistcoat-pocket, sat down at his mother's side, and broke the seal.

"No, no," demanded she, "let me look at the seal, let me see the address and the postmark."

"Mother," said Thor, laughing, "one would suppose you were ten years old. Now come, let us read together; and when I can't make it out, then you shall help me." The letter was written on a large sheet, folded together without envelope, in the old fashion. The father glanced down the whole sheet, turned over on the next page, then to the first again, and finally began : —

"My dear Father and Grandmother —"

"The blessed child, the blessed child!" interrupted the latter, already wiping her eyes with her apron, and nodding her head.

"Hush now, you must please be quiet for a minute."

10

"My dear Father and Grandmother : Hurrah ! here I stand, with the gold medal in my hand, and my head dizzy with the glorious thought of two years of foreign travel. Alone did the poor boy set out in quest of his beautiful princess, and long was the way. Perhaps even his father and his mother, and every one he loved, sent him, if not a curse, at least a pitying smile or a shoulder-shrug, for company on his journey. They knew nothing of his princess, and cared to know nothing. But the boy knew her, and knew that she was to be his. Many strange creatures did he meet on his wanderings. Both Necken and the Hulder, and numberless trolds, large and small, sat waiting for him along the wayside, some to help him, others to do him harm. O, if you could have seen the Hulder of my heart ! She it was who taught me the way to the mountain. Now I can discern the luminous path that leads to the castle where sleeps the beautiful princess.

"An hour ago I stood with some twenty others in the vestibule of the Academy, awaiting the final declaration of the prizes. My heart was now

in my throat, now in my boots, and everywhere
else, except where it ought to have been. The
stairs and the square were crowded with people,
and we twenty culprits stood there, heated and
anxious or shivering, according to each one's
particular temperament, but struggling hard to
look unconcerned. The rest is to me like a dream. ·
I only know that I rushed out desperately, hugged
to my heart the first man I happened to meet,
which fortunately was Vogt, and now I sit here
trying to make you believe that all this is not a
fleeting vision, but true and sober reality.

" I need not write more, for I shall soon be with
you. In two days I shall start on a pedestrian
journey with Vogt, for the purpose of studying
our great mountains and glaciers with my new
eyes. Vogt will visit the parsonage. His father,
who is a clergyman and an old college friend of
our pastor's, once spent some time in our valley,
and, I believe, knows the Henjum people quite
well.. Promise me, however, that you will tell
no one that I am coming. I have my own rea-
sons for wishing it to be a secret. How happy

I shall be to sit once again on the hearth in our cottage and hear once more grandmother's old stories; for grandmother must tell them all over again! My affectionate greetings to you all, father, grandmother, the birch-trees, and the old cottage.

"Your son,

"GUNNAR THORSON HENJUMHEI."

"Heaven be praised," sobbed Gunhild, who toward the close had found ample use for her apron, — "Heaven be praised for all its dispensations, both good and evil. Yea, God knows we have mourned enough for the blessed child. And now he will come back. O yes, I knew he would come home again, I always knew it! You well remember what I used to say to you, Thor. 'Thor,' I would say, 'the boy will soon find —'"

But Thor had already betaken himself to the river, where he still sat poring over his letter, and reading it half aloud to himself; while Gunhild indefinitely continued her soliloquy, with only the pines and the birch-trees listening.

XIII.

RHYME-OLA'S MESSAGE.

T was of course not long before the rumor of Gunnar's great good fortune spread through the valley, from one end to the other, and, as rumors are wont to do, expanded on its flight into fabulous dimensions. Among the first whom it reached was Rhyme-Ola, and it is doubtful if Thor Henjumhei himself rejoiced more in it; but Rhyme-Ola had his own way of showing his emotions; on this occasion, it is said, he danced, laughed, and wept, and on the whole behaved so that people thought he had gone mad. The next thing he did was to appoint himself the sole authorized bearer of the message; and, beginning at the eastern end of the valley, he wandered from farm to farm and from cottage to cottage, proclaiming the great tidings.

Old Gunhild Henjumhei had grown quite lame and stiff of late years, and had not been able to move about much. But as next Sermon-Sunday approached, she began making extensive preparations in the way of arranging and increasing her wardrobe.* For to church she would go on that day, she said, whether she should have to creep or to walk. "And my best red striped skirt, which has lain so long at the bottom of my chest, I shall then put on. For I want to look my best, for the blessed child's sake. And if I were you, Thor, I certainly should have a new jacket made before Sunday. You have worn this quite long enough now."

Thor, after some faint resistance, had to yield the point. And the Sermon-Sunday came. Most of the people had already arrived, and stood in scattered groups, talking by the wall or in the church-yard, when Thor came slowly marching in through the gate, with his old mother leaning on

---

* One minister in the distant valleys of Norway is often the pastor of two or three parishes, and officiates at different times in different churches. Thus only every second or every third Sunday may be a " Sermon-Sunday."

his arm. He looked neither to the right nor to the left, but walked straight toward the church-door. But Gunhild protested. "Wait a moment, Thor," demanded she, half aloud; "I am an old woman, you know, and cannot trot along as fast as you perhaps would like. Let us rest a little here, as other people do, to greet friends and neighbors." Thor had again to yield, though this time rather reluctantly; for to him the attention they attracted had no part in the joy he felt for his son. Not so with Gunhild; she was not loath to receive her due share of the public notice. They stepped into the small paths between the graves, and walked over towards the southern gate where the women were standing. There they stopped, and Gunhild leaned against the white stone fence. Four or five elderly women came up to speak to her. Two of them were gardmen's wives. Thor withdrew to join the crowd which stood nearest. All eyes were turned on him as he approached.

"Well met, Thor Henjumhei," broke forth a chorus of voices. "And thanks for last meeting," added two or three men, reaching him their hands.

" Well met," said Thor, shaking hands round, " and thanks to yourselves. A goodly number of church-folks to-day," continued he ; " more than I ever remember to have seen in harvest-times."

" A pastor like ours is well worth hearing," replied a tall, grave man, who stood next to him.

" They say your son has come to great honor in the capital, Thor," cried a high-pitched voice from the opposite side of the crowd. It was Peer Berg, the father of the " Wild-Ducks."

" About the honor I know but little. He has struggled bravely, and has had the luck with him, God be praised."

" The rumor goes that the king himself has spoken to him, and promised to send him to Roman-town and German-land," ejaculated one, who evidently made some pretensions to a knowledge of geography.

" If that were true, I should most likely have heard of it," was Thor's reply.

" Is it not true either," asked Peer Berg,

"that he gained all the biggest gold and silver pieces in the Ca-Ca-Camedy, or whatever you call it, and that all in one rub?"

Thor answered something, but "the iron tongues of the steeple" spoke with a mightier voice; the air quivered as with full-throated song, and he listened, and forgot what he was about to say. The crowds broke up, and scattered; and with slow and solemn tread the people drew toward the church-door. Soon the church-yard was almost deserted; the entrance-hymn was already streaming out through the open windows, when Thor and Gunhild had reached the door. Then a pretty young girl, in her Sunday dress, with rich, sunny hair, came quickly up to them, looked rather shyly around her, and seized Gunhild's hand and shook it. "I also wanted to shake hands with you," said she, dropping her eyes, and looking on the ground. For a moment she stood still, holding the old woman's hand, and hesitating, as if she wanted to say something more, then again dropped it, and vanished through the open door.

"Bless the child," said Gunhild, "she certainly had something on her heart."

The girl was Ragnhild Rimul.

Walking home from church that same Sunday, Ragnhild met her mother's brother, Atle Henjum. He was just coming down the hillside from Rimul, and had probably been paying Ingeborg a sabbath visit. He gave her a friendly nod as she passed. There was nothing unusual in Atle's going to see his sister; and still, without knowing why, she felt strangely oppressed after having seen him. And then that nod; he usually took no notice of her whatever. When she gained the Rimul gate, an unaccountable anxiety took such possession of her that she had to stop to compose herself before entering. The yard looked scrupulously swept and clean, as it always did on Sundays; but to-day it bore a most distressing air of awkward, self-conscious stiffness. On the staircase of the stabur, or store-house, sat her mother feeding the poultry, but, as Ragnhild felt, evidently waiting for her to come home. As she came within sight, Ingeborg rose and beckoned to her. The poultry knew her too well to mind her presence. Only the cock laid his head on one side, and looked up at her with a knowing air, as if to make her understand that he was well aware of what was coming.

"What was the text to-day?" asked Ingeborg, as her daughter stood before her.

"About the Pharisee and the Publican," answered Ragnhild.

"And what did the pastor say?"

"Well, I could hardly tell, but it was uncommonly fine, everything he did say."

"Much church-people?"

"A great many." Ragnhild was still standing in the yard, her mother a few steps up the stairs. She fixed a strange, searching glance on the daughter, and that firm decision in the lines about her mouth gradually relaxed into an anxious, quivering doubt.

"Ragnhild," said she, suddenly, "you do not tell half of what you think." Ragnhild raised her large, innocent eyes in wonder, but as they met her mother's a deep blush stole over her cheeks; bewildered, she dropped her hymn-book and handkerchief, and quickly stooped down to recover them. It was a good while before she found them.

" Ragnhild," said Ingeborg, with an unusual tremor in her voice, " come into the stabur here, child, and let me speak to you." And she opened the heavy iron-mounted door, and Ragnhild followed. It was a large, spacious apartment, lighted by a few small, barred openings high up on the wall. All around the room stood bins, filled with grain of various kinds, and from the ceiling hung, in long-continued rows, hams, and pieces of smoked and salted beef. But what especially attracted the eye were three huge chests with vaulted covers, elaborately carved and painted, and exhibiting the likenesses of mermaids, dwarfs, trolds, and other fabulous creatures. Through all these fanciful surroundings could clearly be traced the shapes of four or five letters, probably the initials of some long-deceased ancestor or ancestress of the

Henjum and Rimul families. The widow took
the young girl's hand, and led her up to within
four or five steps of the chests.

"Daughter," said she, solemnly, and pointing to the middle one, "can you read those
letters ?"

"L. A. S. H." whispered Ragnhild.

"And those other letters underneath," continued the mother.

"R. S. D. H."

"Do you know what they mean ?"

"No."

"Ragnhild, Ragnhild," exclaimed the mother,
dropping her hand, and with arms akimbo placing
herself right in front of the culprit, "do you
mean to say that you do not know the names
of your own grandmother and grandfather ?"

Ragnhild remained silent.

"Then," continued Ingeborg, indignantly, "it is
high time that you should know them. Those
letters above stand for the name of my father,
Lars Atle's Son Henjum, and the letters underneath stand for the name of my mother, from

whom you were called, Ragnhild Sigurd's Daughter Henjum.   It is strange that her father's name
also was Sigurd. · For now, as you know, those
names will soon again be united."   Ragnhild
stared in hopeless bewilderment on the ominous
letters, as if but dimly divining their hidden
meaning.   Seeing that she had failed to make
herself understood, Ingeborg quickly drew a large
bunch of keys out of her pocket, and opened
the three chests.   Then she raised the covers,
and without delay disclosed their hidden treas-
ures.   There were silver spoons, with large crowned
balls at the end of their handles; curiously
wrought brooches and silver breastplates; a fine,
glittering bridal crown (an heirloom from immemorial times); heavy, snow-white linen for table-
cloths, sheets, and female apparel, all covered with
a perfect maze of elaborate embroidery; skirts and
bodices of darker and brighter colors; and numerous other articles, such as ancient wealth and
family pride hoard up from generation to generation.   While the widow sat deeply engrossed in
the contemplation of her riches, and with evi-

dent satisfaction surveyed, unfolded, and displayed every separate article, Ragnhild stood still aghast, gazing in mute astonishment. Now and then her features lighted up for a moment at the sight of some rich garment or ornament, but soon again were overcast, as by coming evil. Having finished all her preparations, Ingeborg beckoned her daughter to come nearer.

"Child," said she, passing her arm round the young girl's waist, and dropping her voice into a gentle whisper, "do you know to whom all these things belong?"

"They are yours," murmured Ragnhild.

"No, child, they are no longer mine. I have no heir but you, and all that has hitherto been mine is now to be yours." And she raised her head, and gazed into the daughter's countenance to see if she were not overpowered by such a prospect. But Ragnhild's features betrayed no pleasurable emotion; a shade of painful disappointment flitted over the mother's face; she ran her hand across her forehead, and stooped forward as in deep thought. Then suddenly a new idea struck her.

"Come, child," said she, "let me see how this bridal crown will fit you. It is a beautiful crown. I have worn it once myself, and my grandmother and my great-grandmother before me." So saying, she placed the crown on Ragnhild's sunny head; the latter smiled faintly, and mechanically submitted to her mother's strange freaks.

"And then this bodice, and this breastplate," cried Ingeborg, with renewed hope, "they will fit you within a hair, and be so becoming." Ragnhild made no motion to accept the proffered gifts; she stood as if petrified.

"Mother," said she, at length, "pray tell me, what does all this mean."

"What does it mean?" asked the widow, astounded, dropping the breastplate in her lap. "Well, I thought you were old enough to know what it means to put on a bridal crown. However, the case is simply this. My brother, Atle Henjum, while you were still a child, asked your hand for his son Lars. To me, of course, nothing could be more desirable than to see you, my only child, so honorably matched and so

well cared for. Therefore I gave my consent.
It was this I wished to make known to you
to-day. Atle Henjum has been here this morning and has renewed his offer. He wishes the
wedding to take place soon, and I have long
been of the same mind. You are no longer
a child now, but a grown woman. At twenty
I was married myself, and it is my belief
that that is the right age to marry."

The words hummed and buzzed in Ragnhild's ears ; she heard them, but they were to
her only so many sounds, without any special
import. Now they seemed to come floating
from far away, sometimes to ring piercingly
through her torpid senses, and then again they
receded into a dim distance. She marry Lars
Henjum ? She certainly had heard some parish talk about that long ago, — O yes, so very
long ago, she thought now ; for the idea was
as strange to her as if she had never heard
it. And Lars, how ugly he looked to her, with
his broad, ox-like brow and dull, staring eyes !
And her thought grasped despairingly for Gun-

nar ; for in all the fairy-winged dreams which
had risen from her soul in the summer stillness he had been her lord and hero.

"Well," continued Ingeborg, having still received no answer, "you now know my will. It
can certainly not be any great surprise to you.
But with regard to the time, and some few other
things, I should like to know what you think."

There followed another long painful silence.
Ingeborg stared, she knit her brow ; a deep
crimson shot over her face, even up to her head-
gear.

"Ragnhild Rimul," cried she, with rising indignation, "if you have so far forgotten your
birth and your mother's name as still to remember that wandering beggar and vagabond,
whose shame — "

"O mother !" implored the girl, and burst into
tears. But the widow, — she clasped her hands
over her forehead, pressed them convulsively
against her temples, stooped down and hid her
face in her lap ; and a heavy, struggling moan
was the last farewell to a mother's life-hope.

When she again lifted her eyes, Ragnhild was gone.

The maids wondered much that day what had become of the housewife. They searched the house, the barns, and the fields, but they searched in vain. Toward evening they found her again, sitting in her accustomed seat at the south window, and the old silver-clasped Bible lay open before her. But no one durst ask when she came, or where she had been. She glanced up whenever the door-latch moved, then again bent over her Bible.

What were your thoughts then, Ingeborg Rimul? Why did your stately figure stoop, as you staggered from the stabur over to the house, hardly able to bear the burden of your self-wrought grief? And when you opened the Holy Book and sat down to read its well-known pages, why did those words, given to console the afflicted, refuse to comfort thee? Ah, Ingeborg Rimul, it was not the Word of God that was foremost in your mind that night. No, you remember still how your wayward thoughts wandered back to a time which you had long vainly striven to forget. And that moonlit summer night returned to your memory, when you sat under the birch-tree at the river, and your golden head rested lovingly on his bosom. Ah, if he, — if Thoralf Vogt had known of all the weary, sleepless nights that followed those days of bliss; if he could have counted the tears that flowed from your eyes, Ingeborg Rimul, before your faith and your hopes were crushed,— then, you thought, he would not have given you up so easily. But you have changed much since those days. Then your faith in man and God was strong, for you loved as only a nature like yours can love. But, as I say, you have changed much; now you think you can repair one sin by adding to it another, and a greater one: you sacrificed your own happiness, now you offer upon the same altar the life of your child, Ragnhild, your only daughter.

XIV.

AT THE PARSONAGE.

HAT should she do, where should she go?" These were Ragnhild's first thoughts, as, after a short flight upward through the birch-grove, she sank down under a large drooping tree, hid her face in her lap, and wept and wept, and could never weep out her trouble, for the more she wept the more she felt the need of weeping. And the slender birch-boughs waved and trembled; then a faint rustling would steal through the fluttering leaves, as if the tree were trying to hush its own emotion. Hard by stood a steep, half moss-grown rock, over which the water came trickling down in slow, strange, forest-like silence; and a clear pool underneath peered upward with its calm gaze. But Ragnhild wept, — wept until the tears dimmed even her grief, and she at last hardly knew why she was weeping. Her thoughts had wandered far that day, no wonder they were weary. Hush! what a song-rich soul has the northern forest! And its life itself, — what a full-swelling tide of melody! But that was not the voice of the forest. She raised her head, wondered and listened. A strange, soft crooning seemed to grow out of the silence, and then fade into silence again. Suddenly the thought of trolds and elf-maidens flashed through her mind. She sprang up and ran, until she plainly heard somebody calling her name. She paused and looked timidly around. There sat Rhyme-Ola upon the rock, swinging his ragged hat in one hand, and a bundle of papers in the other. It was plainly the papers he wished her to see; for as she hesitated, he flung his hat away, and again waved them towards her.

"Ragnhild," cried he, "was it not what I always used to say?"

Ragnhild took a few steps toward the pool, smoothed her hair, and washed off the marks

of her tears ; then by the aid of a small birch
and some juniper-bushes, climbed the rock to
where Rhyme-Ola was standing.

" It was the very thing I have always said,
Ragnhild," repeated he, as if he were taking
up the thread of a conversation which had been
broken off a minute ago.

" What is it you have always been saying,
Rhyme-Ola ? " asked Ragnhild, astonished, as,
flushed and panting, she gained the singer's lofty
haunt.

" Take a seat, make yourself at home," said
he ; " I am going to tell you all about it."

She dropped down upon a stone and sat looking expectantly into his face.

" You remember," resumed the other, " how
often I used to say that the valley would hear .
of him when they least expected it."

Ragnhild had no recollection of such a proph-
ecy on the part of Rhyme-Ola, but, hardly
knowing what he meant, she answered musingly, " O — yes " ; then, suddenly throwing herself
forward, added in breathless haste, " And what
have they heard of him, Rhyme-Ola ? "

"Look here, Ragnhild," cried her companion,
gayly, "if you have not heard strange things
before, you may be sure you will hear them
now. It was only what I always said ; but
nobody would believe me, not even you, Ragnhild."

"Yes, yes, I *do* believe you," exclaimed the
girl, impatiently. "Only pray tell ; what is it
you have heard?"

Rhyme-Ola took one of the papers he held in
his hand, unfolded it, and handed it to Ragnhild.

"You will find something there," said he ;
"I can't read, you know, so I can't tell you
where it is. The pastor told me it was there.
He gave me the papers yesterday, and I promised him to carry them to the judge for him ;
for they two keep the papers together. But I
have been keeping them to show them to you,
Ragnhild, for I knew that, next to myself, there
was nobody in the valley who would care more
to see it."

She did not seem quite to catch his meaning ; she opened her mouth, and the question

she was about to ask — well, she did not exactly forget it, but it just vanished on her lips, and she did not know what had become of it. So she sat there only gazing on Rhyme-Ola, but said not a word.

"Well, well, Ragnhild," said he, visibly disappointed, "if you don't care to read it, I am sure I sha'n't urge you." And he reached his hand out to take the paper back again; but she snatched it, then sprang up, and down she ran over the steep hillside, so loose earth and bowlders came rumbling after in her track.

"Ragnhild, Ragnhild, don't you hear, it is the pastor's paper," cried Rhyme-Ola. A heavy bowlder with a fierce rush dashed against a huge-stemmed fir. That was all the answer he got. A minute after he saw her light figure vanish in the dense birch copse below.

Since the time of her confirmation, Ragnhild no longer slept in her mother's room. Up stairs in the eastern gable of the house, a little chamber had been fitted up for her, and a very pretty chamber it was. It was five years now since she was confirmed, and still the girlish pride she took in her little bower was as fresh as the first day she entered it. She had spent so many happy hours up there. The furniture was perhaps scanty enough; but it was all, if not more than she required. Near the door stood the large painted chest in which she kept her wardrobe; then a bed in the wall, which, however, no one could see, unless when the trap-door was opened through which she entered it; but the door was generally open, and the snow-white sheets, the sheepskins, and the rag blankets which Ragnhild herself had woven were always in such perfect order that she hardly would mind, if you stepped near and took a look at it. The walls, which had retained the natural tint of the wood, were decorated with a small looking-glass, a colored print of Prince Gustaf, and the following verses painted in red letters, one at the head and the other at the foot of the bed : —

"May the good God look on me,
Keep my sleep from evil free;

Cleanse my soul from sin and shame;
So I sleep in Jesus' name.

"Thou hast waked me, God, from sleep;
Thou this day my feet wilt keep.
Glad to labor I arise,
Under thy protecting eyes."

When Ragnhild woke up the next morning, her first thought was the newspaper, which she had hid under her pillow; but the wish she made when she did it, she would not for any prize have told to living mortal. She again examined the paper, read the article through, word for word, to assure herself that it was all true, and that she had not merely dreamed it. The words "art" and "artist" struck her singularly; Gunnar was an artist, it said. What was an artist? She had some faint notion that his pictures might have something to do with it, in fact, she knew they had; but the word was strange to her, and she had no very definite idea of what it meant. She rose and went with one of the maids to the cow-stable to milk the two cows they kept on the home-pasture, then helped

in scouring the milk-pails; but still the word
"artist" haunted her, and would let her have no
peace. She must find out what an artist meant.
Suppose she asked Thor Henjumhei? No, that
would never do; he might suspect more than she
wished to betray. But the old pastor, — he was
the very man; learned was he, so he would be
likely to know, and a better man to come to
in trouble there never was. It never had happened before that Ragnhild had forgot her work
or left it half done; but this morning it did
happen. Ingeborg opened her eyes wide, when
she saw her spring out of the gate with her
Sunday skirt and bodice on, and lightly dance
down the hillside towards the river. "Well,
well," muttered she, glancing at the half-scoured
milk-pails on the hearth-stone, "if that were what
I had taught *my* daughter! But when one
stone loosens and rolls, then the whole heap
will be sure to follow. Alas!" added she, with
a sigh, "I am afraid that child will do me but
little honor."

It was a clear, sunny summer morning. In

the pastor's study windows and doors were thrown wide open, and the sunshine glinted through the blooming apple-trees in the orchard into the little room, where the worthy clergyman sat at his desk poring over some documents connected with the poor-fund or some other equally distracting matter. Again and again he allowed his pipe to go out, turned the papers over and over, and scratched his head in a kind of comic despair whenever a new difficulty presented itself.

A slight knock at the door called the pastor's attention from his papers; he glanced up, and saw a fair young maiden standing in the hall waiting to be admitted. He rubbed his glasses, put them on his nose, and looked at her.

"Ah, Ragnhild Rimul!" cried he, agreeably surprised. "Come in, my child. You are very welcome. You do not at all disturb me; you need have no fear of that. Come in. How is your good mother?"

Ragnhild in the mean time, after having made a deep courtesy to the pastor, had found a chair

at the door, where she sat down, modestly looking on the floor without saying a word.

"And your good mother is well, my child?"
repeated the old man. Ragnhild stammered
something to the effect that her good mother,
when she saw her last, was enjoying her usual
good health.   The pastor expressed his gratifi-
cation at so desirable a state of affairs, and
hoped that the daughter also was enjoying the
same blessing.   Now, here was a chance for in-
troducing her question, but Ragnhild felt so
bashful and embarrassed that she could do nothing but twirl and twist the corners of her apron,
and hardly knew herself what she wanted to
say.   Indeed, she had talked frankly with the
kind old man so many a time before, and had
never felt the least hesitation.   She had always
had the most unbounded reverence for him, and
had been used to think that, next to God, there
was none who knew more than he.   To-day was
the first time she had anything she wished to
hide from him; and it was this which made her
heart sink, as her eyes met his.   In this minute

she had a vague sensation that he already must have discovered her secret, and she was ashamed of herself for ever having wished to keep it from him. He saw her embarrassment, and tried to come to her assistance ; but she heard nothing of what he said. Then he also was silent, and although she still sat gazing on the floor, she could feel his eyes fixed steadily on her. She must speak. And she summoned all her courage, gave her apron a desperate twist, and, in a voice half choked by the tears, suddenly broke out : —

" Would n't father please tell me what it means to be an artist ? "

And with a powerful effort she swallowed her tears and tried to look unconcerned.

" What it means to be an artist ? " said the pastor, with ill-concealed astonishment. " My dear child, what have you got to do with artists ? "

" Well, I just wished to know," answered she, boldly, but pressed her hands against the chair, and set her teeth firmly the moment she had spoken ; for, in spite of the warmth, they seemed alarmingly disposed to clatter.

"An artist? Well, to be an artist is to be engaged in the study of Art, whether it be Architecture or Music or — But perhaps you will have some difficulty in understanding—"

Ragnhild certainly had difficulty in understanding, which he, in fact, did not wonder at. And mistrusting his own information on the subject, he arose, pulled a large volume of his Encyclopædia out from the bookcase, and without further introduction began to read. But one regiment of big words marched up, followed by another of still more promising dimensions, until at last even the pastor despaired, and shut the book in disgust. Having put it back in its place, he went up to Ragnhild, stopped in front of her, and looked at her in wonder.

"My dearest child," said he, tenderly, "if you are in trouble or distress, be assured that I shall be glad to do anything in my power to help you. You know you can trust me, child, do you not?"

That was too much for a poor overburdened heart. "Father," cried she, "I am so unhappy," and a shower of tears nearly choked the confession, "I love Gunnar so much. I always did love him. But mother does n't like him, and she calls him a beggar and a vagabond, and that hurts me so much. For you know he is no vagabond, father, and not a beggar either."

"Yes, dearest child, I know. A nobler and worthier youth our parish never bore."

"That was what the paper said too," sobbed she, — "and then it cannot be a sin to love him, can it, father?"

The pastor made no answer. She stayed her weeping, and lifted her tear-filled eyes on him imploringly. It was not in his power to resist.

"No, child," said he, warmly, "it is no sin to love. And," added he, after a moment's pause, "if ever a youth was worthy of a maiden's love, he is."

"O, thank you, father!" cried she, "for that was the truest word —"

"Your mouth ever uttered," was what she was about to say, but suddenly remembering that that would not be a proper thing to say to her pastor,

11*

she restrained her joy, and after some hesitation continued : " I was so afraid that I might be wrong! but now, when I know that you also think what my love for him had early taught me to think, I shall nevermore be in doubt — And if you would please tell my mother so, she would also learn to think differently, for she would believe you, father, although she would no one else."

The pastor folded his hands on his back under his dressing-gown, and began walking briskly up and down on the floor. There was no denying that his sympathy for the poor girl was strong and heartfelt ; and he now suddenly discovered that he had allowed his warm heart to run away with his judgment. Of course, he was not ignorant of the Henjum and Rimul marriage-scheme, and even if he had been, it would be unpardonable in him, as a minister, to encourage a daughter to rebel against her mother's wish. "Alas !" sighed he, "I always find myself running into this kind of scrapes. How often shall I suffer before I learn ? And what is now to be done ?"

A thought struck him. Ragnhild was well versed in her catechism ; he could refer to no higher authority. So he stopped again before her. " Thou shalt honor thy father and thy mother," said he, slowly and solemnly, "that it may go well with thee, and thou shalt long live in the land."

This done, he again resumed his walk, and, having found a new argument, again stopped.

" He that honoreth not father and mother — "

His eye met a sweet, puzzled look in her innocent face, and he had not the heart to go on. Then a faint smile flitted over her features, for her quick eye had already told her where his sympathies were in spite of the stern words of the law. It is indeed inconceivable where she found the courage to say what she did say, and she often thought so herself afterwards, but as the answer came to her, she had already uttered it before she had time for a second thought.

" Thou shalt obey God," faltered she, "rather than men." It struck him singularly to have the ignorant peasant-girl meet him so promptly on his own ground. It was now his turn to look puzzled. He dropped down in an easy-chair at the desk, laid his hand on his forehead, and sat long as if in deep thought. Ragnhild, fearing her presence might be unwelcome to him, arose and walked toward the door.

"I hope you will excuse me if I have disturbed you, father," said she ; "farewell."

"Stay, child, stay," demanded he, without changing his attitude. And she remained standing at the door, looking at him, and wondering what he could be thinking. And the silence lasted a long while, until at length she feared he had forgotten her altogether. She took a few steps toward the writing-desk, made a deep courtesy, and said : —

"Father, I think my mother will miss me if I stay longer."

Then he arose, grasped the hand she reached him, and with warmth and earnestness said : —

"Ragnhild, if you have failed to get the help and the advice you might justly expect from me, as your pastor, you will not think that it has been from any unwillingness on my part, or from indif-

ference to your welfare. Perhaps it rather was
because I felt too much for you both. But the
matter you have mentioned to me to-day is one in
which no human helper will avail you. Therefore
pray to God that he will help you, and act then
in accordance with what your own conscience tells
you to be his will, and you will never go astray.
And now, child, may God bless you! Farewell!"

Ragnhild would have thanked the old man if
she had been able. As it was, she could only fal-
ter a faint farewell, and hurry out into the clear,
sun-teeming morning. He went to the window,
lit his pipe for the twentieth time, and saw her
skipping down the road past the little white church,
until the forest and the distance hid her from
his sight.

"Ah, yes, yes," murmured he, "it is the old,
old story."

XV.

THE RETURN.

E who has seen the bird of passage only in a comparatively southern latitude, can form no idea of the wildness of rapture with which it hails its return to that far land where the blooming meadow and the eternal glacier lie basking together in the wealth of the summer day, and where the forest breathes its fairy life under the burning dream of the midnight sun. To the minds of many the name of Norway suggests a picture of winter-clothed pines and far-reaching snow-fields, with little or no relief from the influences of the gentler seasons; and still, strange as the assertion may sound, Norway is peculiarly the "Land of Summer." There is no doubt that the birds at least think so, and their testimony is likely to be

trustworthy. And he who stands in the glory
of the morning in the heart of one of the blooming fjord valleys, hears the thousand-voiced chorus
of the valley's winged songsters welling down
over him from the birch glen overhead, sees the
swift, endless color-play of the sun-smitten glaciers, the calm, lucid depth of the air-clear fjord,
and the trembling frailty of the birch-bough under the sturdy strength of the fir, — ah! he
whose gaze has but once dwelt upon all this will
need no other persuasion than that of his own
eye to unite in the song of the thrush and the
cuckoo and the fieldfare about the peerless beauty
of Norway's summer. It is not heat that makes
summer; its life is of a far subtler and more
ethereal essence. Who knows but the glacier
itself may do its share toward intensifying this
life, or at least our own perception of it? For
the white, snow-peaked background, with its
remote breath of winter, grazing the horizon
of the mind, sets summer off into stronger and
bolder relief. And if the bird feels and rejoices
in this, how much more should the artist!

It was just on one of these wondrous summer mornings that Gunnar, after more than three years' absence, saw his native valley again. He and his friend Vogt had arrived the evening before at a little fishing-place on the other side of the fjord, and had immediately engaged a couple of boatmen to carry them over. Already the sun stood high; it was about five o'clock. The boat shot in through the fjord, gliding swiftly over the glittering bays, in which rushing mountain streams mingled their noisy life with the great stillness, and forest-clothed rocks and headlands stood peering forth through the morning mist, which still hung in a kind of musing uncertainty along the shore, while the fjord lay wondering at the endless caprices of glaciers and sunshine. A few stray sea-gulls kept sailing in widening circles round some favorite fishing-haunt, calmly judging of the prospects of the day, and now and then with slow deliberation grazing the surface of the water, as if to convince themselves that it was not ether, but the veritable element of the cod and herring. Silent families of loons and eider-ducks rocked on the motionless deep, but vanished quick as thought when the boat approached.

They were already in sight of the Henjum shore, when the scream of a gull awaked Gunnar from the delightful revery in which he had been indulging. He had been sitting so long, looking down into the fjord, that for a moment he was quite confused, and hardly knew whether to seek the real heavens above or below. Now he stood erect in the stern, and with a bosom swelling with hope and joy saw the dear scenes of his childhood emerging from the fog and the distance, and smiling to him in the full light of morning. There was no denying that he had changed considerably in the three years he had been away. The cut of the features is of course the same; the strength of contour in chin and brow are perhaps even more prominent than before; while at the same time the lines of the face seem refined and softened into a clear, manly expression. That dreamy vacancy in his eyes which had once distressed his grandmother

Q

so much is now supplanted by the fire of lofty
purpose and enthusiasm; but the confident open-
ness, which to Ragnhild's mind had been the
chief characteristic of the Gunnar who went,
she should not seek in vain in the Gunnar who
had now come back to seek her. The city dress,
which at the request of his friends he had assumed
on entering the Academy, would, at least in the
eyes of the parishioners, by an added dignity
more than compensate for its undeniable inferiority
in picturesqueness. However, the broad-brimmed
Panama hat and the large traditional artist neck-
erchief gave him a certain air of brisk activity,
which accorded well with his general bearing,
even if the light summer jacket and city-cut
pantaloons did not show the plastic shape of
the limbs to the same advantage as the national
knee-breeches of the valley.

Vogt, Gunnar's friend, was a great patriot.
And as he often used to say himself, no one
can be a good patriot without loving the nature
of his country, or, in fact, all nature both in his
own country and elsewhere. But as long as we

are all flesh and blood, weariness has also its
claim upon us, and even Vogt, in spite of his
patriotism, had for once been obliged to recognize this claim. For sleep is rare on foot-jour-
neys, and has to be taken at odd intervals, whenever an opportunity presents itself. Thus it
happened that Vogt at this moment lay stretched
out on a blanket in the bottom of the boat,
and slept, quite regardless of his companion's
rapture and the beauty of the morning. Now
the rowers drew up their dripping oars, while
one of them sprang forward to ward off the
shock against the pier. Gunnar seized a rope,
which hung from the flag-pole, and with a leap
swung himself up. Vogt, who had just been
forcibly recalled to consciousness, chose the safer
method of climbing the staircase. He was a
tall, slender youth of twenty, with a fine open
countenance bearing the marks of earnest appli-
cation and hard study; he wore spectacles, and
the traditional Norwegian college cap, with its
Minerva cockade and the long silk tassel. His
complexion was perhaps a little paler and his

hair a little darker than is common among Norsemen.   Gunnar had already climbed more than half-way up the slope of the Henjum fields before Vogt could find a chance to speak to him. For, although the collegian strode along at his highest speed, he had not yet overtaken Gunnar, and would probably not have done so, if the artist had not at this point found something which peculiarly arrested his attention.

"Vogt," cried he to his panting friend, "there you see the twin firs."

"The — twin — firs," repeated Vogt rather hesitatingly, but then suddenly correcting himself. "O yes! I should have imagined them to look somewhat like those.   What majestic crowns!"

Gunnar made no reply, but seemed to take great delight in the twin firs.

"Most extraordinary growth," suggested Vogt; "and that little bench between the two trunks, don't you think it peculiarly invites to rest? What if we accepted the invitation?"

"No; really, you would do me a favor if you would try to walk a little farther.   My home is only a short distance from here."

And on they marched; but having arrived at the Henjum gate, Vogt's strength gave out so entirely that he had to sit down in the grass at the wayside and implore his fellow-traveller, in the Hulder's name, to save the last atom of breath which was still at his disposal. Gunnar had again to check his impatience, and flung himself down at his friend's side.

"Vogt," exclaimed he, suddenly, pointing across the river, "do you see that cluster of houses on the hillside yonder, right under the edge of the forest? Do you know what that place is called?"

"Perhaps I might guess," replied Vogt with a quiet smile; "if I am not much mistaken, they have hitherto borne the name of Rimul."

"How the sun glitters in the long row of windows; just as it used to do of old, when I came wandering up those hills from the river!"

"Sunshine is a good omen," answered the collegian, "especially when it proceeds — But by your immortal Hulder!" (this had of late become Vogt's favorite oath,) "who is that sunny-haired creature who is coming there? Charming! Now be on your guard, Henjumhei, for our adventures are fairly commencing."

Gunnar looked aside, and immediately recognized Gudrun; she was carrying two well-filled milk-pails from the stables over toward the stabur, or store-house, which, according to Norse custom, was built along the wayside. Vogt in an instant was on his feet and ran to meet her. She, seeing him, put her milk-pails down, shaded her eyes with her hand, and viewed him with unfeigned curiosity.

"My fairest maiden," exclaimed he, bowing in the most courteous manner, "you certainly overtax yourself in trying to carry those heavy pails. Would you not have the kindness to permit me to assist you?"

Gudrun's eyes widened not a little while she listened to this speech, and having with a second glance assured herself of the harmlessness of the man, the absurdity of his proposition struck her so forcibly that she could no longer contain herself, but burst out into a hearty laugh, which was echoed from behind the fence at the wayside.

Vogt, who had imagined his deportment the very perfection of gallantry, looked utterly mystified.

"I beg your pardon," stammered he. "I meant no offence."

"Offence!" cried Gudrun, checking her laughter, "who is talking of offence? And if you are so anxious to carry those milk-pails, I am sure I shall not prevent you."

If Gudrun had been shy in her childhood, she certainly must be credited with having now overcome that trait in her character; for there was little of shyness in the way she harnessed the young man up in the yoke, hitched the milk-pails on the hooks, and marched him over to the stabur. But then, she had now been taught for twenty years that she was the daughter of Atle Heujum, and need not be afraid of anybody.

Having, after some difficulties, gained the stabur and successfully landed his burden on the steps, Vogt, in the agreeable excitement of adventure, seated himself on the threshold of the door and tried to open a conversation with his fair unknown.

" I supposed all young maidens stayed on the saeter during the summer months," said he.

"O no, not all!" replied Gudrun, coming out from the stabur with a huge wooden bowl filled with milk. " Would you not like to drink a cup of milk ? I don't know if you like it fresh. This has just been strained."

" Thanks, a thousand thanks ! I like it just this way," cried he, delighted, putting the bowl to his mouth ; " but," added he, removing it, " would n't you pledge me first ? I am sure it would taste much better then." She laughed, drank, and handed him back the bowl, whereupon, having marked the place her lips had touched, he greedily attacked it. " You have not been staying at the saeter this summer, then ? " resumed he, rising to return her the empty bowl.

" Yes, indeed, I have. But my cousin Ragnhild and I take turns at it, and stay at home every other week. Her week will be out on Sunday, and then comes my turn again."

" Your cousin Ragnhild ? " repeated Vogt, astonished.

" Yes ; perhaps you know her ?"

" I have heard of her. And then your name is probably Gudrun."

" Yes ; how do you know ? Who told you ? Do you come from the capital ? Yes, of course you do. And perhaps you have heard of a young lad from our parish, Gunnar Henjumhei by name, who has lately got to be something great. If you have, then please tell me all you know about him."

Gudrun hurried her questions out in an eager, breathless haste. The young man eyed her curiously. " You will excuse me this morning," said he, reaching her his hand, " my time is short. But you will see me again before many days, and then I shall tell you all you wish to know. I have a friend waiting for me out in the road. Farewell."

Gudrun was so astonished that she could not even find words to return his parting salutation. Half an hour later she was still standing on the spot where he had left her, wondering how all this would end ; for she had no doubt that the friend on the road was Gunnar.

12
.

Never had the little cottage at Henjumhei seen a day like this. It was a feast-day, and such a feast-day as had never been before, and would not be likely ever to return. On the bench out under the drooping birches sat old Gunhild, holding the young artist's hands in hers, gazing into his face with tear-wet eyes, and assuring herself that it was just what she always had said, that the blessed child would be sure to turn out right, whatever they said of him. Opposite, on a three-legged stool, sat Thor in his new jacket, quiet as usual and of few words. Still there was none who would have questioned which was the happiest man in the valley that day, and Thor himself least of all. He had taken a holiday, and sat smoking his afternoon pipe. On the ground, a few feet distant, lay Vogt, leisurely puffing away at a cigar, and otherwise dividing his attention between the family and the huge overhanging rock, at which now and then he cast fearful glances, as if he were not quite sure that it was firmly fixed. Gunnar was the one who led in the conversation; for of course he had to tell all that had happened to him, from the time he had left home, and Thor and Gunhild listened with enchantment. It did not escape his observation that, at one or two points in his narrative, his father turned his head abruptly, and suddenly found some interesting object across the river. Vogt also would throw in a remark here and there, either reminding his friend of some important circumstance which had been forgotten, or commenting upon his report whenever he put too modest an estimate upon his own merits. Thus the afternoon passed away, until about five o'clock. Then Vogt announced that he was expected at the parsonage, and Gunnar — well, Gunnar had also an errand which would admit of no postponement.

Ragnhild was at the saeter. To-day was Saturday; her week would be out to-morrow, and then Gudrun would come. There was no time to be lost. A hundred wild longings drove him onward, and, springing from stone to stone, he hurried up the steep mountain-path. It was the path he had climbed so often before; every old fir, every moss-grown rock, he knew. The shadows were growing longer; a lonely thrush warbled his soft melodies

in the dusky crowns overhead; the river roared in
the distance with a strange, sonorous solemnity,
as if it were afraid to break the evening's peace;
here and there the forest opened as by a sudden
miracle, and through the space between the mighty
trunks he could see the peaceful valley with its
green fields and red-painted farm-houses stretched
out in the deep below; a gauze of light bluish
smoke hung over the tops of the lower forest regions; and underneath lay the fjord, clear, calm,
and ethereal, mirroring the sun-warm forms of
mountains, clouds, and landscape in its lucid depth.
It was indeed a sight for a painter; and still
the painter had but little time to bestow upon
it at this moment. The sun already hung low
over the western glaciers, and glinted through
the trees, wherever the massive heads of the
pines opened a passage. The day had been
warm; but the air of the highlands was cool
and refreshing. He had now gained the region
where the heather and dwarf-birch begin to mingle with and gradually supplant the statelier
growth of the forest. The slow measured beat

of the bittern's wing and the plaintive cry of
the curlew were for a long while the only sounds.
Having recognized the rock from which on that
eventful night he had beheld the merry scenes
of the St. John's hill, he could not resist the
temptation to pause and recall the situation to
his mind. Then a clear, ringing yodle, followed
by the call of a loor, shook the evening air,
while the echo answered from all the four corners of heaven. He sprang up, held his breath,
and listened. The loor sounded again, and the
same clear, ringing voice sang out in the four
tones of the yodle, as it were right above his
head : —

"Come, children all,
That hear my call, —
Brynhilda fair
With nut-brown hair !
Come, Little Rose,
Ere day shall close ;
And Birchen Bough,
My own dear cow ;
And Morning Pride,
And Sunny Side ; —
Come, children dear,

For night draws near.
Come, children !"

There never was another voice like that; it was
Ragnhild, calling home her cattle. In the next
moment the highlands resounded with the peal
of bells and the noisy lowing of the cows. Peeping through the trees, he saw her standing on a
bare crag not far above him. She looked taller,
paler, and more slender than the last time he
saw her, but more wondrously fair than even
his fancy had dared to picture her. She held
the loor in her hand, and stood bending forward, and half leaning on. it. Her hair hung in
golden profusion down over her shoulders, and
as the warm rays of the evening sun fell upon
her, it shone like a halo. His first impulse was
to call up to her; but just as he had opened
his mouth, she yodled again, then sang out her
call to the same melody, only substituting other
names, and ended with a long, alluring note
from the loor. Again the echo played with her
voice, the cattle lowed, and the sound of the
bells, the waving of the tree-tops in the under-

wood, and the creaking of dry branches marked the progress of the returning flocks. He bent the dense copse aside with his hands, and began to climb; he saw her glance wandering out over the valley, then farther and farther away, until it lost itself in dim immensity. There was a nameless longing in that look. To him it was a blessed assurance.

"Ragnhild!" cried he, grasping a loose tree-root and swinging himself upward. She paused, smiled, held the hand up to her ear as if to listen. There was no surprise in her smile, but quiet, confident joy. Again her eye sought the distance, as if the distance had given her answer.

"Ragnhild!" called he again, "Ragnhild!" and he was now but a few rods away. She stooped over the brink and saw him standing on a stone below.

"Ragnhild," said he "do you not know me?"

A slight tremor ran through her frame; she looked once more, then in her bewilderment turned and started to run. But swifter than

thought he was at her side, and held her hand
in his. A deep crimson gushed over her cheek,
and from under the drooping eyelids a tear
stole down and lighted on the blade of her silver brooch.

"Ragnhild, dearest," cried he with sudden fervor, "have I changed so much for the worse
that you no longer know me?" And waiting
no answer, he flung his arm round her waist
and drew her closely up to him. She let her
head fall on his shoulder, and gave free course
to her tears.

"But, Ragnhild, beloved," continued he, setting
her gently down at his side in the heather, "is
this the greeting you give me? Are tears the
only welcome you have for me?"

"Gunnar," answered she, now raising her head,
and the brightest smile of happiness beamed
through the tears, "I am so very foolish. But.
then you looked so fine and — and — so foreign
that I knew not what to say, and so I cried."

"Foreign, Ragnhild! Do I look foreign to
you?"

But with the same open, trusting smile she
met his anxious, searching glance, while she answered, "No, Gunnar, not foreign. But you
know I cannot in a moment overcome my wonder; I can only sit and look at you. And if
you knew how I have longed for this day!"

"My fairest, sweetest girl! and you have
longed for me?"

He clasped her in his arms, and kissed her
lips. "You shall long no more now, Ragnhild, for from this time I shall always be with .
you."

She glanced anxiously up into his face, as if
the words suggested something which in her joy
she had forgotten.

"You will always be with me, Gunnar," said
she as if to convince herself, — "always?"

"Yes, beloved. And how beautiful you have
grown, Ragnhild! The same as you ever were,
and still not the same. How many a time I
sat at my garret window in the city, late in
the night, and thought of you and longed for
you! And then often I would say to myself,

'I wonder how Ragnhild looks now, and I wonder what Ragnhild is doing or thinking now.'"

"O, how delightful!" cried she in happy surprise; "why, is n't it strange, Gunnar?—it is the very thing I have always been thinking, when I sat in my window in the gable, and the woods and the fjord and even the river lay hushed into a great stillness. O, how many thoughts of you and longings for you took flight then through the stillness! And whenever spring came, I was always so anxious to hear the cuckoo the first time in the east, for you know that means a wedding. And, do you know, always before, during these years, I would be sure to hear him in the north, which means grief. But this year, when I never thought of it, he sung out in a fir right over my head, and that is the best of all. I sat as quiet as a mouse, and counted on my fingers how long he should sit, while I could repeat my wish three times. And for every time I whispered your name, he sung. Then I was no longer in doubt, for I knew you would come, Gunnar."

And now came his turn to tell the history of his pilgrimage. And he told her all, and in strong, glowing pictures, such as only love can paint, and in words such as love only can utter. When he had finished, she sat still silent, gazing up into the tree-tops, and smiling to herself, as if rejoicing in the contemplation of some happy thought.

"Ragnhild," said Gunnar, "what are you thinking about?"

"Ah," answered she, "I was only wondering at your beautiful words. They flow like a poem."

"And if you could read that poem, Ragnhild," cried he, "you would know that its burden had ever been you, and would ever be you."

XVI.

A SUNDAY AT RIMUL.

O one who was in the habit of visiting
Rimul could have helped noticing how
clean everything looked there. Indeed,
the widow of Rimul had become quite proverbial
in the valley for her tidiness, and people never
talked about it without a sneer; for what business had she to sweep and wash and scour more
than other honest housewives in the parish?
Everybody, of course, had a thorough-going house-
cleaning before St. John's Day and before the
three great festivals of the year, and that, most
women found, was as much as they could man-
age; and what would be the use, then, of wast-
ing one's precious time by distributing through
ten days what might just as well be done all
at once? Thus ran the parish gossip. But the

widow had her own notions on this subject, as indeed on every other, and if she chose to sweep and clean her house every Saturday, she was at all events herself the loser, if indeed there was any loss about it. She had also taken particular care duly to impress this necessity on her daughter's mind; for it had been an ancient usage in the family. "And," said she, "when God rested on the seventh day, it was after having finished the whole work of creation, even to the least blade of grass or fringe of a cloud, and not with some bit of work lying over until next Saturday."

This morning Ragnhild had come home from the saeter earlier than usual. In the large sitting-room with the many windows she found her mother seated at the table, turning over the leaves of her Bible. The floor was strewn with small tassels of juniper-needles, which spread their fresh fragrance through the whole house. In the four corners of the hearth stood four young birch-trees, remnants of the St. John's Day decorations. It was not Sermon-Sunday to-day, so there could be no question about going to church; but on such days it was not uncommon that some one of the neighbors would drop in during the forenoon, and chat with the widow about the state of the crops or the prospects of the fishery. Therefore, said Ingeborg, it was always well to read one's gospel and sermon early in the day, lest, by delaying, one should be altogether prevented from making an appropriate use of the sabbath.

Ragnhild went to the window and stood for a moment looking down the road, then hurried to the hearth, and out of the door to look for something, then forgot what she was looking for, and again returned to the window, where she began to drum on the panes for want of other occupation. An hour passed, but no neighbor made his appearance. Ragnhild grew more and more restless. It was nearly noon when at last steps were heard out in the hall and two men entered. The one was Thor Henjumhei, the other a young city-dressed gentleman. The widow raised her eyes, looked quietly at the men, and remained sitting.

"Good morning, Ingeborg Rimul," said Thor, approaching the table and offering his hand, "and thanks for last meeting. It is blessed haying weather we have had this week."

Ingeborg shook Thor's hand, and returned his greeting. The daughter cast a stealthy glance at the young gentleman, but quickly turned again, and stood pertinaciously drumming on the window.

"Find yourself a seat, Thor," continued the mistress of Rimul; "and the young man you bring with you, it is probably your son, — Gunnar, was n't that his name? — I can recognize him by his likeness to yourself, Thor."

"I hardly think I could have traced that likeness myself," observed Thor; "but they say strangers can see such things better."

"So they say," was the widow's reply.

The worthy houseman in the mean time had taken a seat at the window opposite the widow, and sat leaning forward with his elbows resting on his knees, and deliberately turning his cap in his hands, as if weighing well what he was about to say. The son remained standing. For a long while no one spoke.

"Ingeborg Rimul," began Thor at last, and his eye met the widow's stern glance unflinchingly, "it is about this son of mine I have come to-day to see you."

Ingeborg opened her eyes widely and gazed as if she would gaze him into atoms; but it had no effect upon Thor. He sat there calm and imperturbable.

"It may seem strange that I should come to you on such an errand as the one I have to-day," continued he, "but we have all of us to go through many strange and unexpected experiences before we are done with this world. And you know yourself, Ingeborg Rimul, that he who has but an only child, will do much for that child's sake. Now, what I came to propose to you is this. It hardly can be an unknown thing to you that Gunnar, my son, while he was yet a mere child, took a great fancy to your Ragnhild, and if her own word can be trusted in such a matter, she was not very old when she first discovered that he also had a place in her heart. And this is no longer a trifling, childish affair, now, Ingeborg Rimul; for when love springs up so early and grows with the years, it is hard to root it out. Three years ago I should probably have had many doubts and misgivings before venturing to speak to you of such a proposition; but the son I offer you to-day can speak for himself, and I dare say needs no apology from his father. He has learned his profession well, the newspapers say, and is well worthy of the love of any Norse maiden."

It is difficult to tell how long it was since Thor had made a speech like this; but one idea brought two others with it, and love and a slight but very pardonable feeling of paternal pride lent warmth and power to his words. He did not observe Ragnhild, who, attracted by his eloquence, had approached and now stood on tiptoe only a few steps from him, listening with open mouth and an anxious interest expressed in features and attitude; but Gunnar did see her, and found it hard to check his impatience.

And her mother also saw her, and her heart
grew heavy; for she felt her strength failing
her.

."Thor Henjumhei," said she, with a visible
effort to appear composed, "I do not doubt
that your son is a worthy young man, or that
he knows his profession well. And I feel as
sure as you do yourself that there are maidens
enough who would be more than happy to be
called his wife. But just on this account I
wonder that a man of your sense and judgment
can come here and ask for him what you know
yourself he cannot get. For it must be well
known to you, Thor, that Ragnhild's hand is
no longer her own, neither have I the right to
give it away."

The daughter, knowing from a former occasion her mother's mind on this subject, dared
not interpose, and she turned away and wept.
And Gunnar? Well, under such trying circumstances he may perhaps be forgiven for forgetting the rules of parish propriety; for when
the sunshine, after a minute's absence caused

by ·the passing of a cloud, again visited the large sitting-room, the widow of Rimul rubbed her eyes and would gladly have persuaded herself that she was not quite awake; but there was no denying that, as the sunshine stole in through the south window, it found the heiress of Rimul with her hands clasped round the houseman's son's neck, and with her sunny head closely pressed to the houseman's son's bosom.

"Thor Henjumhei," cried, Ingeborg, helplessly, and rising from the table, "take your son away!"

But Thor did not stir.

"Thor Henjumhei — "

Then there was a knock at the door, but no one answered; the door opened, and in came a tall, slender youth; he stooped a little, wore spectacles, and had the long-tasselled college cap in his hand.

"Mr. Vogt," said Thor, "I am afraid you have come here in an unfortunate moment."

"I am exceedingly sorry to hear that," replied Vogt, "and if my presence is inopportune — "

But the widow of Rimul, — what has happened

to her, with her eyes riveted on the new-comer, and that ghastly paleness of her visage?

"O God, my God!" groaned she, sinking down into the nearest chair, "thou hast visited me hard. Thy will be done." And Ingeborg buried her face in her lap, while the tears fell fast from eyes to which they had long been strangers,—only God knows how long. There was a solemn stillness in the large sitting-room.

"Children," said the widow at length, — and as she lifted her tearful eyes Ragnhild, her daughter, and Gunnar, the houseman's son, stood before her, — "may the Lord bless you now and forever! And if I have struggled long and hard against you," added she, taking their right hands and joining them together in hers, "think not that it was because my heart was against you."

Then Thor, old Thor Henjumhci, stretched out his rough hand to the widow of Rimul, and the widow grasped it, looked into Thor's faithful eye, and shook his hand heartily.

"Ingeborg," said Thor, "God bless you for that word."

But Vogt, — how did he account for all the commotion occasioned by his arrival? There he stood in the middle of the floor, with a blank, bewildered stare, turning now to one, now to another, but unable to utter a single syllable. Vogt knew not, perhaps, that in the widow of Rimul's eyes he resembled his father as one drop of water resembles another; neither did he know what long-buried memories those well-known features called back to the widow's mind. So he remained standing as if he had dropped down from the clouds, until at last old Thor, seeing his helplessness, rose, and came to his assistance.

"Ingeborg Rimul," said Thor, taking the collegian by the hand and leading him up to the mistress of Rimul, "this is Mr. Vogt, a young collegian, and the friend and benefactor of Gunnar, our son."

Then Ingeborg grasped the young man's hands, held them long in hers, and gazed earnestly into his face.

"Mr. Vogt," said she, and she paused, as if the word sounded strange on her lips, — "Mr. Vogt, your features were once familiar to us here in the valley. I bid them welcome again, and hope this will not be the last time they are seen at Rimul."

Vogt stammered something about his pleasure at being present on this happy occasion ; then Gunnar and Ragnhild came up and joined in the conversation ; and, before long, the happiness they all felt loosed their tongues and made each one feel at home with the other.

Thor, in the mean while, had despatched a boat for his old mother, and the widow of Rimul had sent a horse and a carryall to receive her at the landing-place down by the river.

Old Gunhild soon made her appearance, whereupon followed a little scene such as only grandmothers can act, and none but a *genre*-painter can depict.

It was about this time that the pastor, who had been preaching in a neighboring parish, came riding past the Rimul buildings, and, as it occurred to him that it was a good while since he had paid the widow a visit, and that he was much in need of a glass of milk to slake his thirst, he dismounted from his horse, hitched it to a post at the wayside, and in another minute entered the well-built mansion. The Rimul yard was in its usual holiday trim, everything in its place, and the staircase and the hall fragrant with the fresh juniper. There was certainly nothing unusual in this, and still, as he stood in the hall, the pastor could not rid himself of the impression that something extraordinary had happened ; but when he opened the door and found the Rimul and the Henjumhei families gathered as in council round the big table at the south window, when he saw Thor seated at the widow's side, and Gunnar whispering in Ragnhild's ear, what need had he then of any further explanation ? But the pastor was too much of a diplomat to betray that he was previously informed. He had already resolved to afford every one the satisfaction of being the first to proclaim to him the happy tidings.

And no sooner had the worthy clergyman entered the room than the widow herself, with not a little pride and formality, informed him of the happy occasion of their rejoicing ; told him, what

he already knew, of Gunnar's wonderful proficiency
in his art and great prospects for the future, and
finally requested the honor of his company as well
for this evening as for the wedding, which, according to agreement, would take place a month from
date. It is needless to add that the pastor's kind
face then beamed even more than usual, and that
he congratulated both the old folks and the young
with a deep-felt earnestness which went to the
heart as surely as from the heart it came. And
when at the supper-table he gave the toast of the
betrothal, and spoke of the sacredness of love, of
the triumph of native worth over prejudice and
all obstacles, and of the great and holy mission of
the artist,. then tears glistened in the eyes of all,
their cheeks glowed, their hearts beat more quickly,
and they were all happy.

But when the supper was at an end, — the ale
drank, the toasts finished, — when the sun grew
red and weary, as evening was sinking over the
valley, and the peace of evening into the hearts
and minds of all, then Gunnar and Ragnhild sat
together on the bridge of the barn out in the yard,

and saw the gold of the sunset burning on the far steeples of the mountains.

" Do you rémember, Ragnhild," said he, letting his fingers glide through her rich hair, while her head rested on his shoulder, " I think it was on this very spot, about fourteen years ago, when I first met you, and — "

"O yes," answered she, dreamily, "the time when you asked me if I were the Hulder."

"And you were my Hulder, Ragnhild," said he, earnestly, and pressed her more tightly to his heart, " my fair, my good, my beautiful Hulder."

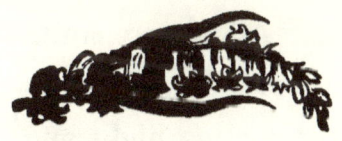

XVII.

THE OCEAN.

AUGUST has come. The fjord still lies glorying in the life of the summer, the sunshine glitters still in the clear waters, the light birch-tree stands trembling over its frail image in the cool tide, the thrush warbles in the mountain glens, and the screaming hosts of sea-birds drift round the lonely crags, or stream over the heavens with the ebbing and flooding sounds of huge, airy surges.

There is life on the fjord in August, a teeming, overflowing life. All nature smiles then; but in its very smile there is consciousness of decay, — a foreboding of the coming night and of the heaven-rending November storms.

Yes, August has come, — come to the fjord and to the valley and to Gunnar and Ragnhild. She is no longer Ragnhild Rimul now, she is Ragnhild Henjumhei, the wife of Gunnar Henjumhei, the artist. And no one would have doubted that she was Gunnar's wife who had seen the two together that night, when they left their native valley ; for it was much that she left behind, — mother, home, and country; but, thought she, it was more that she had gained. Now it was morning, or rather night, for the sun had not yet risen. The wheels of the steamboat lashed the water into foam, as it rushed onward and onward through gulfs and straits, onward in its way to the ocean.

At the prow of the steamboat stood Gunnar Henjumhei and his wife, she leaning on her husband's arm, and now and then glancing half timidly back at the dear old glaciers and mountain-peaks, as they faded one by one on the far horizon. His eye was turned toward the future, peering steadfastly through the light fogs of the morning.

" Gunnar," said she, and a half-sad, half-happy smile flitted over her features, " how strange to be leaving all behind me that I know, and to sail out into a great foreign world, where all is unknown to me, — except you!" added she in a whisper. And as the thought grew upon her, she pressed the arm she held, and clung more closely to him.

"Ragnhild," answered he, "it is not a foreign world. But see how the great sun is rising — over the ocean."

And he pointed toward the east, where the sun rose — over land and ocean.

THE END.

www.ingramcontent.com/pod-product-compliance
Lightning Source LLC
Chambersburg PA
CBHW020857020726
47497CB00005B/1451